Death Is a Drum

. . . beating forever

By John Wyllie

DEATH IS A DRUM . . . BEATING FOREVER
TO CATCH A VIPER
THE BUTTERFLY FLOOD
SKULL STILL BONE
THE GOODLY SEED
DOWN WILL COME THE SKY
RIOT
JOHNNY PURPLE

Death Is a Drum
...beating forever

JOHN WYLLIE

PUBLISHED FOR THE CRIME CLUB BY
DOUBLEDAY & COMPANY, INC.
GARDEN CITY, NEW YORK
1977

All of the characters in this book are fictitious, and any resemblance to actual persons, living or dead, is purely coincidental.

ISBN 0-385-12783-9
Library of Congress Catalog Card Number 76-50872

Printed in the United States of America
First Edition

For Mairuth

Death Is a Drum

. . . beating forever

No man can threaten, or argue back, from the grave.

The little girl had hair the colour of new manilla rope. It was parted in the middle and combed out into two ponytails which stuck out on each side of her head above and behind her ears. The ponytails were tied with pieces of striped red-and-white ribbon.

She was talking to herself aloud and in Dutch. At the same time she was building a little model of an African village, with red mud for the walls of the huts, twigs for roof beams, and a sort of esparto grass to represent the thatched roofs.

"The Chief has four wives," she told herself, "so he has to have six huts in his compound. One for each wife, one for himself, and one as a greeting hut. Then there will be a roofed kitchen area so that the women can cook when it rains and have someplace to store the corn. They are going to be difficult to build because . . ." On her last visit to her grandparents in Holland she had been taken to see the scale model of a Dutch town in Madurodam and had been enthralled by it.

A shadow fell over her village from behind and she looked around. The person to whom the shadow belonged was not a total stranger to her, because as she went back to patting a mud wall into shape she switched to Fulani, the language of the nomadic herdsmen who range all across West Africa with their cattle.

". . . because they will have to be raised off the ground. Oh Fulani one," the child said without looking over her shoulder again, "this is not a village for such as thee. See, I built it with mud walls which last. Thou hast not the need for walls which last. Tents, or at best huts made with grass, are all thy people use. Is that not so?" She was ten years old and she had been in Fort Etienne for four of those years, was going to be an ethnologist like her father, and spoke

Fulani because they were the people on whom he was writing a book at the same time that he lectured at the local University College.

"Thy people have much to answer for, oh Fula," she continued. "It is thy cattle, sheep and goats which make the land bare so that it turns to desert. Thou and thy ancestors before thee. My father says of your herders that . . ."

Her words ended in a small, curious sound which was squeezed out of the back of her throat. Then she threw herself on her back, clawing at the nylon line which was biting into her neck. With her back arched and her hips off the ground, pivoting on her shoulder blades, she kicked herself around in a full circle while her head obliterated the model village she had been building.

She was less than a hundred yards from her home. The ground she had been playing on lay behind a line of huts where the houseboy, the cook and the gardener lived. There were no back windows in the huts, so there was only one pair of eyes to watch her die, the murderer's.

The child's eyes, unlike those which were fixed unemotionally on her, were blue, and after a few moments they were empty and staring up at the sky, which was also blue and empty.

After the little girl's body had been motionless for a while, the killer picked up the large, empty waterpot she had set down earlier and put it on her head, balancing it effortlessly, though it was on its side and placed so that its length projected beyond her shoulders.

Then she walked back unhurriedly the way she had come a bit earlier, passing the half-built but abandoned house from which she had watched patiently for the opportunity to make her kill.

Later, the same woman was waiting some way down a dusty track that turned off the main east-west road which passed through Fort Etienne. The waterpot was now full and weighed over a hundred pounds. She had carried it on her head from a public standpipe in the strangers' zongo on the west of the town, where another Fulani woman had helped her to lift it high enough so that she could duck underneath it, get it balanced and straighten her back. She had walked almost two miles, her neck muscles ached and she was sweating heavily.

She had seen the green truck driven by the Master near the central market, and the fact that the then-still-empty pot had pointed over her right shoulder had told him that she had been successful in the task he had set her. She also knew that he would pick her up soon.

He would be pleased with her. They would celebrate. It would be the fifth celebration in as many weeks.

The Master expected obedience to his wishes, immediate obedience, yet he was much more than a severe disciplinarian. He gave the lives of all his women a meaning they had never expected to find. To most men they were beasts of burden in between the times when they were not bearing children. He brought them excitement and gave them a sense of importance, though both feelings were tinged with fear. To almost all of them he was God, Allah, who was compassionate and merciful but also possessed of "strong fetters and flaming fire." The Master was the spirit of the great winds which, at times, blew out of the east for days on end, teasing and tormenting.

She would be alone with him in the truck for the rest of the day. They would camp for the night, just the two of them, and she would burn with a different kind of fire born of ecstasy, not fear.

Hassan ben Salah M, the Master. His brother was called Arrani M, and his sister Kali M. Arrani was strange, thin and nervous. He was also of her own people. Kali had long fingers with long fingernails and used them like knives to dig the truth out of the other sisters at Alamut. She was to be feared, that one, feared as one feared a witch.

One feared the Master as one feared a lion.

All three of them burned with yet another fire which the others knew from its strange heat to be foreign, yet when the Master turned it towards them the women burned with it, too. Then it was so bright that they could see and feel nothing else.

It had burned in her until the child with the straight hair that was the colour of the sun . . . was dead.

The fire in her had made her want to do more, to do greater violence, but the Master had told them all that the pain of a hundred pricks with a needle which drew little blood was greater than that of a cut with a knife from which the blood flowed freely. Their object was, he had explained, to cause pain which led to fear. Fear had to be planted and tended carefully. If the pain becomes too great the victim may lose consciousness and therefore cease to feel pain and fear. In the case of the child, one of the sisters had said, it was a pity no blood would be spilt because the blood of a child would be sweeter than that of an adult, like the flesh of a lamb is sweeter than the flesh of a sheep.

The Master smelled of his strength, which was the smell of a stallion.

Kali used much strange perfume which came out of bottles, and often changed from one day to the next.

Smells were important because they had very little water at Alamut.

She, the water carrier thought, would wash tonight with some of the water she was carrying on her head. The Master would want her to be clean before he bedded her. She could use the same water he would use after he had finished with it.

She stopped walking and looked slowly around, slowly because the great weight on her head was inert, and once it started moving it was hard to stop. The full pot of water ruled her movements at that moment like the Master ruled her life.

Beyond the cultivation around the outskirts of the town the land was bare of vegetation except for a few tufts of elephant grass, some spiky camel thorn, and two baobab trees. This area was to the northwest of the city. In the other areas there was guinea corn and rice, because the fields could be irrigated from the Niger.

Where the woman stood now the land was largely made up of flows of flat rock with occasional puddles of dusty soil that were too shallow and too small to be worth cultivation. It was the bones of the earth which were visible here, brown old bones that had been polished by the everlasting wash of wind and sand which at times seethed over the rocks with the force of flood water. On the faces of the rocks which were turned towards the east this wash had smoothed and rounded the surfaces, its main force being derived from the harmattan, which filled the sky, right up to the sun, with the dust of the Sahara.

To the man driving the mammy wagon, a local style in trucks, the distant silhouette of the girl with the waterpot on her head spoke of victory, or at least another step towards it. She also spoke of femininity, the desirable and the desired. Beyond that, there was the thought that her loins, which would give him children, would also give him the means to celebrate his victory. She was graceful, submissive, and he had taught her to be deadly. When he was honest with himself he also acknowledged that she could use her sex to bait him and to tantalise him, though only, he told himself, when he was in the mood to be tantalised and baited.

Anyway, it was Kali's job to see that the women knew their places and did not overstep the limits. Kali, the Goddess of Death, ceremonial death, when she stopped playing, stopped putting on a fireworks display, her venom became cold-blooded and vicious. The women said she became bewitched and turned into a hyena. The two women who had lost their sense of submissiveness and obedience and had had to be killed, had certainly looked, in the end, as if they had been killed by a hyena.

Yet the fear which had been generated by those two ritual killings was not the dominant feeling at the caves of Alamut. Most of the time they were a family, his family. Fourteen women, fifteen with Kali, and two men.

Kali would not be with him tonight, only the Fulani princess, "Broad Tail."

From experience he knew all his women's behavioural characteristics when he brought them to the peak of sexual gratification. This one became like a wildcat, with every muscle and nerve in her body jolted by massive electric shocks.

Broad Tail. He had given them all names like that, names which they had inherited, though none of them knew it, from the Sultanas of Pulaski and Sixteenth in Chicago.

He brought the truck to a halt beside her and got out to help her out from beneath her head load.

They put the pot of water in a specially made holder in the back of the truck. He had designed the holder himself to cushion pots of water against the shocks and vibrations of cross-country travel.

Broad Tail. He smacked it playfully and told her to put it in the front seat. Normally she would have ridden in the back. Trying to take advantage of his obviously favourable attitude towards her, she took his hand and tried to pull him off beside the road, smiling. He shook his head, and though she pulled with all her strength, digging her heels in the sand, he did not move. He said, "Later."

"Now. I am hungry now."

"Later. We are too close to the town. Get in."

He spoke to her in her own language, haltingly, not as accurately as Kali or Arrani could have given the order, yet with more authority than either.

That he did not speak the language as well as they did, did not bother him.

He was the Master, and no one except Kali or Arrani was allowed to speak to him directly. No one in Africa ever spoke to a chief directly, only through a linguist. Arrani was his linguist.

Only after she had asked his permission, when they were alone together, might one of the women speak to him directly. Broad Tail had not asked for permission. He would beat her a little when they stopped for the night, to remind her of her omission, even though he was pleased with her. Or perhaps it might be because he was pleased with her and wanted to add a little zest, for both of them, to the pleasures which would follow the beating. He tightened his jaw muscles as he thought of the "exercise" which lay ahead.

Like all the women of her people, his companion wore a sheet of white cloth which fell to just below her knees. It was held in place by a mere twist of the material as it overlaid the fold beneath it. Over her head she wore another length of white material, which fell over her shoulders like a veil. All he had to do to bring her out of her white chrysalis was to release the twist of cloth and pull the veil away from her, and a black Venus would stand revealed before him.

He wore white, too. Yards of the stuff worn over a short white tunic, and loose trousers held up around his waist by a drawstring. Part of the outer cloth was wound around his head and shoulders so that he could adjust the folds, when there was dust in the air, to keep it out of his nose and mouth.

Soon the track they were following would run out at a place where, after the rains, there were a dozen acres of foodstuff for cattle. After that, there was no route for him to follow and he would be dependent on his knowledge of a few landmarks, a boulder of a certain shape, a wadi where for a few days after a rainfall there might be water, the skeleton of a cow which must have strayed from the herd and become lost, a small cluster of date palms growing by a hole which gave brackish water, and finally, depending on the degree of visibility, a distant view of the massive pile of boulders towards which he was heading.

It was a journey of over one hundred fifty miles across shale, sand and great slabs of rock. By dragging bundles of camel thorn behind the truck he managed to erase, to all but the most discerning eye, any tracks the wheels of the truck left in the patches of sand.

At sunset they had camped, and before she had surrendered willingly to what had been no more than a symbolic beating—she had continued to smile all through it—and he had rewarded her for having accomplished the task he had given her, she cooked supper and they ate it. This time, however, she had remembered her etiquette and had waited until he had finished eating before she, herself, had started to eat.

Afterwards he left her lying beside the embers of the fire while he went and sat on a rock a little way away.

Nowhere else that he had ever been were the nights like this. People who lived on the world's shoulders talked of there being stars in the sky as if they knew how many billions there were. Here around its belly it was possible to see them. There really was such a thing as starlight, and it was possible to drive the car by it without having the headlights on.

When he had belonged to the Sultans, a gang of kids who had terrorised fifteen blocks of Chicago's black ghetto, he would never have believed that one day his territory might be measured in hundreds of square miles and that it would be on the southern fringe of the Sahara. Had he known it, it would have given him something to dream about during the several short periods he had spent in the penitentiary.

Later, after he had been drafted and sent to Vietnam, there had been other things to occupy his mind. It was there that he had found himself as a man and had risen to the rank of sergeant. "Natural leadership capabilities"—that was what his discharge papers had said he possessed. He had "belonged" there in his unit in a way that he had never belonged anywhere else. The others in the unit, who had not had to "make it" on the street corners of a ghetto as he had, did not know their way around like he did. The squad had belonged to him and had depended on him for many things they could not get or do for themselves. He could out-talk and out-manoeuvre the General himself, was what they had said of him. And he had depended on their dependence on him.

After the end of the war, however, there had been nothing.

No place to live except back in the ghetto, no job for a twenty-eight-year-old veteran who had been in the "pen" before the war, even though he had two purple hearts and "natural leadership capabilities." Especially, there was no place where he could exercise those capabilities legitimately.

So he had had to make a place, whether it could be called legitimate or not.

He could use a gun. He had been able to do that as a member of the Sultans before they gave him an M16 and taught him to kill as a profession. In Chicago the intent had seldom been to kill, any more than it was in any run-of-the-mill street fight.

Causing the death of other humans had only come to mean something to him in Vietnam. Then it had developed a real purpose, that of bringing him out on top in any given situation. No man could threaten, or argue back, from the grave.

He had learned, too, that the men who had given him the job of killing in the name of justice were as vulnerable to death as gooks, when you could make a case out against them for being as unjust as they had been to him and millions of other blacks. When you killed them you also came out on top, as he was beginning to prove. The trick was in the way you went about the job.

Yes, he could kill, and he knew a trick or two about the way to do it. Operation "Depurate." He could plan an operation and name it, too. He was going to clean up the world by getting rid of all the white trash.

He had shown everyone that he could plan an operation . . . and a very profitable one. Like over a million and a half dollars' worth of good planning. And that was just the beginning.

From a comparatively small investment in three handguns, it had built up to that nice fat figure in a little over four years. The difference between his operation and those of most others, who had had the same background as he had had, was that he had something else to do with the money than just spend it. The difference, in short, was the ability to use a gun to kill rather than use it only to look important and make a noise.

They, he, Arrani and Kali, had started out with a couple of well-planned payroll holdups. Then a really big, smart job on a bank. After that, they had netted enough to get out of the country and down to Jamaica. There they had picked up some new passports and had gone on and repeated the exercise in British Honduras, picking up another set of passports there. In both places they had lived very quietly, careful not to draw attention to themselves. Their only real outlay in money, in fact, had been for the passports.

Their main activity during those months had been to stoke up the fires of their hatred for white men, compiling a dossier such as the police might put together on a gang of criminals.

After that had come the really big one.

Dateline: Liberia. Roberts Field. A Boeing 707 on a charter flight full of wealthy American Rotarians making it around the world.

They did not get past their second stop.

With a gun in her back, the girl who operated the information desk had put out a call for six of the most important passengers who were the leaders of the group. When they turned up, they found that the message waiting for them would be spoken from the barrel of a gun if they did not do as they were told by the gunmen.

The order they were given was to tell everyone to go back on the plane and that if there were any empty seats when the two men and the woman who were holding them hostage came on board, they would start to shoot, killing their hostages first. Five minutes for the operation to be completed was the time limit that he had set. The first of the passengers he had spoken to had refused, and at a nod from him, Kali killed the man, blowing a hole in his head. The gunshot had been heard all over the airfield on the Tanoy system. The next one to be told to speak had a gun jabbed savagely in his ribs, so that the open mike caught his cry of pain. Threatened with the same treatment again, he said, "This is Larry Emmett, folks, and we are caught in a holdup. They just—Jesus—they just killed Cy Brookman and they are going to kill the rest of us if you all don't do what they want you to do. And that goes for the crew, too. Here's what it is . . ." And he repeated the orders he had been given.

The surprise factor had been their greatest asset. No one had had the time or the capability to think of any effective countermeasures.

The ship's crew had been ordered to join the others in the passenger cabin, and this action had been followed by, in the first place, cleaning up all the spare cash and jewelry which people had with them and, secondly, the setting of a ransom figure for the plane and its complement of men and women. So that it could be paid quickly, they had been careful not to set the figure too high. A cool million dollars cash in small denominations had been the demand, and two hours the time limit set for the authorities in Monrovia to get the money to them. After that, he had declared, there would be one passenger killed every fifteen minutes until the money and an airport bus were delivered.

The press had made quite a feature of the fact that the two passengers whom he had had to kill before the ransom finally arrived had been volunteers, a widow and a widower.

After that, the money arrived and they had moved another dozen passengers to the bus and, having warned the authorities not to have them followed, had had the driver take them northeast out through the American-owned rubber plantations to where they had a well-stocked truck being guarded for them by a small-time local smuggler.

Before they left the bus, Arrani had taken the armature out of the magneto.

Everything, all the way through the operation, had gone exactly to plan and night was falling as they left their hostages, with one woman being violently sick, evidently from relief. From there they had headed off along a bush trail towards the nearest frontier.

By the time they stopped they had crossed three frontiers, driving at night along trails which were shown to them by their tame smuggler, who thought he was going to become one of the gang and get his hands on part of the loot.

Then they went to ground for six months in Port St. Mary while the smuggler got their passports doctored with the necessary visas and entry stamps.

While they had lain low, he and Kali had learned to speak Fulani and had, later, tried out the garrotte he had devised on the smuggler, who was beginning to increase his price for his services beyond what had seemed to be reasonable for what he delivered.

The garrotte, like the hijack, had worked perfectly, and they had disposed of the man's body where it would quickly be made unrecognisable by vultures.

At the end of six months, having changed their appearances to match the photographs on their West Indian passports—for the men this had meant shaving off beards, and for Kali the abandonment of a wig—they had driven north to Transniger, quite openly, along the main highways, the Big M and Kali posing as visitors making a tour of the lands from which their ancestors had been shipped as slaves, with Arrani as their guide. At no time did they spend any of the ransom except for a few dollars here and there with Yoruba traders whose operations as money changers were also illicit.

Progress to the point where he had finished phase one of his plan had cost the enemy only three lives. They had been lucky. The price of vengeance had so far been very small.

Now they were into phase two, and everything was still going smoothly with the score at five down and fourteen to go.

One of the toughest jobs in the beginning had been recruiting women.

African social structures were tightly knit and well-cemented together by tradition.

They had needed strays and dropouts and had found them principally in two sets of circumstances which were in extreme contrast to each other—in the universities, and in the disaster areas of the Sahel, particularly Transniger itself. Kali had done the recruiting on the university campuses amongst the female dissidents and extremists who formed the majority of the "family." Arrani had bought a few young women in the Sahel for sacks of rice and other foodstuffs. Of course, it had all been done with great care and caution so as not to arouse the suspicion of the authorities.

After Kali and Arrani had brought the girls in, he, the Big M, had taken over, working individually on each girl according to what he felt were her needs. Primarily his objective had been to establish his own authority as the leader of a fanatical and mystical cult. In this he had been successful, partly due to the intensity of his own feelings about the crusade he saw himself leading, partly the hunger which had led him to read a scrambled mass of literature which included the Koran, *Theories of Primitive Religion, The Autobiography of Malcolm X*, along with *I Ching*, the Tarot, the *Tibetan Book of the Dead*, works on scientology, the Kabbalah and anything else which came his way and dealt with religion, the occult, secret societies and books that related to violence, murder and terrorism. He had started all this reading in the penitentiary during his youth and had taken it up again in the West Indies, in Akhana, and now in Transniger.

With his family of women, his own sexual vitality, his physical strength, and his ruthless determination gave additional force to the power of his fanatical belief that Operation "Depurate" had the validity of a total and final solution to the curse that Yokub's devils—Elijah Muhammad's name for white men—had inflicted over hundreds of years on black men.

All this gave him the right to be called the Master—or the Big M, as Kali and Arrani called him—by the rest of the family.

Though he had not personally participated in the killing of the child earlier in the day, she would still have been alive if he had not decreed that she should die. So another stone had been laid in the foundation of the structure which would eventually carry his name down the ages, and to that extent a small part of his sense of mission was fulfilled.

Turning his face up to the stars, he closed his eyes and tried to clear his mind to let in another thought that was aggravating him. He concentrated, made an extra effort, and the would-be interloper revealed himself.

Doctor Quarshie. A newspaper had said that the authorities were going to employ Doctor Quarshie to investigate the murders.

How good was the man, really?

However brilliant or capable, and even though he was black, he was mortal, flesh and bone. He could be stopped. He, the Big M, could come out on top of him in the same way that he had come out on top of everyone who had got in his way since he discovered the finality of the solution which death imposed on problem makers. There would be no future to the man's investigations beyond the grave. He, Arrani and Kali, would have to get together over the Tarot cards and see what they had to say about the illustrious Doctor.

Crystalising it brought the thought clear of his mind, amputating it painlessly. It would give him no further anxiety until he decided to give attention to it again.

He went back to the girl, woke her, and to show his contempt for anyone who thought that they could cause the Master to doubt his capabilities, he exercised his mastery over her again, which gave her a quite unexpected bonus of satisfaction and delight.

ONE

. . . this particular garrotte had been designed by someone who intended to make a profession of murder.

The slim, middle-aged African driver sat at the steering wheel of his vehicle with the pride of an aristocrat, knowing there was no one who was his superior. All his attention was concentrated on what he was doing, yet he had an air of nonchalance, expressed by his immaculate white cotton gloves and by his easy mastery over the superannuated Greyhound bus as he guided it over the narrow strip of blacktop road which ran all the way from the seacoast of Akhana, for five hundred miles, to the Sahel and the Sahara.

Along the edge of the road, where the tar met the loose sandy soil, the soft shoulders had been chewed ragged by the wind and by the rare rain which, when it fell, created instant torrents on each side of the attenuated highway. In many places there were deep potholes and wide patches where the surface of the road had melted away down to the thin rubble which acted as metalling. The driver, however, kept his vehicle moving as steadily on its course as if he were driving on a turnpike rather than on a road that was not only threadbare but coming apart at the seams.

Watching him, Doctor Quarshie felt that the man deserved recognition, if only because he so successfully made a very difficult job seem very simple. It was also clear that the man's equilibrium had been undisturbed by his discovery at the last stop that one of his passengers, a white man—the only white man on the bus—had been murdered, and the garrotte that had been used to kill him had been left in place around his throat.

Quarshie wished that he could treat this fearful discovery—he had been called immediately to make an examination of the dead man—with as little concern as the driver was showing. Then he reminded himself that he was involved in the murder in a way in which the driver was not. Or, at least, he had to assume that he was involved and that the man's death was connected with the other murders he had been persuaded to investigate by his old friend the French Ambassador to Akhana, the country in which Quarshie made his home.

Three white men had already been killed in Transniger in the same way that the white man had been killed on the bus. Transniger is a country which lies in the Sahel region of West Africa. It shares a common frontier with Akhana, and its bleak countryside was slipping past on each side of the bus as Quarshie was engaged with his thoughts at that moment. General Magalabakar, the President of Transniger, was also an old friend of the French Ambassador to Akhana and had appealed to him to persuade Quarshie to help the Transnigerian authorities in their efforts to trace and capture the killers.

Now, as if to flaunt their contempt for the man the General had called in to search for them, the assassins had committed a fourth murder no more than a few feet away from the seat in which Quarshie had been sitting for the past fifteen hours.

Tired and made uneasy by these thoughts, the Doctor turned his attention away from the driver to watch the dawn pushing the hood of darkness westward across the sky. He also saw the growing light force long jagged shadows across the otherwise flat terrain from the bizarre, slag-heap-sized piles of rocks which dotted the landscape and from occasional baobab trees with their tentacle-like branches and their grotesque trunks, which always looked to him as if they had a bad case of elephantiasis.

When the rim of the sun appeared above the horizon the driver brought his bus to a stop and more than a dozen passengers got out. Each in turn washed his face and hands in a cupful of water he took from a special container provided by the bus company, and then knelt or stood beside the road to make the obeisances towards Mecca.

Other passengers also took the opportunity offered by the stop to walk a little way into the savannah, on the other side of the bus from the Muslims, to relieve themselves.

A few remained in their seats, and somewhere amongst them all, Quarshie thought anxiously, there is a murderer who, during the halt when everybody except the white man had left the bus to drink midnight beers or to quench their thirsts in other ways, must have returned to the vehicle, approached his quarry from behind, dropped an expertly made noose over the man's head and then pulled it tight.

The weapon, or tool—Quarshie was not sure what to call a piece of nylon fishing line—was expertly made. It had toggles at each end, a brass hook a little way in from one of the toggles on one end of the line, and a number of eyelets attached to the cord that were spaced out from its centre towards the other toggle. Thus, the murderer could drop the garrotte in place, pull it tight, slip the hook into the appropriate eyelet and escape, leaving his quarry to struggle briefly and futilely until the pressure on his carotid arteries caused him to black out and then, in a few minutes, to die because his blood circulation had been excluded from his brain.

It was also possible that his death might have been caused by the pressure the garrotte had exerted on his vagus nerve or by strangulation. The latter case could not have occurred in this particular instance because the cord had not slipped above the hyoid bone, nor, as far as Quarshie had been able to tell, had the thyroid cartilage been fractured.

Unless help came very quickly, it was impossible for the victim to escape, because he first had to pull the cord tighter still in order to disengage the hook from the eyelet. For a man struggling with death to tighten the garrotte was more than could be expected of anyone, even if he had known that he could free himself in that way.

When he had first examined it, after removing it from the victim's throat, Quarshie had decided that this particular garrotte had been designed by a man who intended to make a profession of murder. Its main assets, from a killer's point of view, were that it enabled the assassin to get away from the scene of his crime as quickly as he could have had he shot his victim, and it gave him an advantage over a killer with a gun because death caused by a garrotte came quickly, certainly, and almost silently. It seemed to Quarshie that the thing was a measure of the criminal or criminals he was up against. It had about it all the beautiful simplicity which usually comes with a thoroughly functional design—and this was the element which had been discomfiting him ever since he had been brought back from the roadside shack and his bottle of beer to look at the dead man. It seemed as if the assassins were waiting for him and had killed right next to him to show that they could have got to him just as easily with their secret and soundless weapon.

Or were all these assumptions he was making invalid? Quarshie wondered. Was the fact that the murder had been committed on the same bus on which he was travelling just an accident? And had someone else refined the garrotte long ago to make it such a perfect tool for those who wished to use it to kill?

He turned his thoughts back to the dead man. He had been talking with him earlier during the ride up through Akhana, and had actually sat next to him for a couple of hours as the bus had made its way north through the rain forest and up onto the plateau which took them into savannah country.

A more unlikely victim for an assassin would be hard to find. He had worked, the man had told Quarshie, for a Catholic relief agency and had been on his way back from an international meeting of relief-agency people in Port St. Mary. He had been—and now was no more—what is known amongst white West African expatriates as an "Old Coaster," that is, a European who has lived a large part of his life in the region. He had also been, Quarshie decided, a well-intentioned, compassionate man who had learned to love West Africa and its people without, however, really overcoming the paternalistic attitude that was common to so many expatriates of his generation, background and experience.

Of course there could be no denying the effectiveness of the attitude adopted by the whites for so many years in West Africa. At the point of guns and machine tools, they had manoeuvred the native Africans into a position from which the black man had had to accept the whites' claim to being the "master race." In fact, just how deeply this feeling had become ingrained in the African psyche had been shown earlier in the evening by an incident which had occurred on the banks of the Niger and had involved the man whose body occupied the seat behind Quarshie.

A pair of bridges, which connected Akhana with Transniger via an island in the middle of the river, served both railway and motor traffic, the latter travelling on planks that were set on railway sleepers both between and outside the railway lines.

The bus had crossed the first bridge onto the island, but had then been held up behind a long line of traffic at the entrance to the second bridge. The story being told by the other drivers was that work was being done on the structure and that it was temporarily closed to motor traffic.

After about half an hour, when there had been no movement of any of the trucks, cars or buses, a small group of passengers led by a lawyer and including a couple of young doctors, a bank manager, and the owner of a textile mill, had got out of the bus and had walked the quarter of a mile to the bridge to determine exactly what was happening. After a little while they had come back bitterly angry because the engineer in charge of the work, who was an African as they were, had dismissed them peremptorily, when they had asked how long the work was going to take, with the words, "Three weeks."

To cross the river by the next bridge meant making a detour of over four hundred miles and possibly having to back the bus over the first section of the bridge, which was only a little wider than the bus itself and had no guardrails.

When the delegation from the bus had returned to it defeated, the white man had said to the lawyer, "But my dear fellow, that's ridiculous. Do you mind if I trot up there and have a word with this engineer chap?"

Of course, no one had been able to object to the man's offer, and a little later the bus had moved to the head of the queue and, with the white man standing up beside the driver, the barrier had been lifted and the bus had proceeded across the bridge.

The Muslims, having completed their prayers, returned to the bus, and as it moved forward again Quarshie decided that the loss of face suffered by the Africans, owing to the white man's success, was not, in itself, motive enough for murder, even though some of the passengers may have felt sufficiently shamed and savage to wish the man, and all like him, dead.

However, if that was not the motive, who, Quarshie wondered, out of the thirty-eight passengers on the bus, could possibly have had a reason to kill such an inoffensive man?

There was still over an hour before the bus was due to arrive in Fort Etienne, and Quarshie debated whether he should try to question the people on the bus. He was not, however, taken with the idea. The bus driver and perhaps a few Akhanaians knew who he was and why he might take it on himself to question people, but it was something the Transnigerians might not know and would therefore resent.

He had been told that a Transnigerian official would meet him at the bus station when he arrived. Therefore, the right thing for him to do, he decided, would be to tell the bus driver to use his authority to hold the passengers on the bus. This official would then be the one to question the passengers, perhaps with some help from Quarshie.

The thought still nagged him, however, that now was the time when some sort of action should be taken. At least, he decided, he should have a look at his fellow passengers and try to memorise the faces of any of them who aroused his suspicions.

He was sitting in the front seat of the bus nearest the door, with the dead man stiffening into rigor mortis in the seat behind him. The toilet being at the rear of the bus gave him an excuse to walk back down the aisle towards it, scanning the people on each side, thinking that if the man was an Akhanaian he might make him feel uneasy and therefore look guilty. It was a somewhat artless approach to the problem of finding a man who might be making a profession of murder, Quarshie conceded, but at least it was better than sitting and doing nothing.

The bus had just passed through one of Transniger's larger towns, and the quality of the road between there and the capital improved enormously, making the rolling and shuddering of the vehicle much less violent than it had been for most of the trip. It had crossed Quarshie's mind, as they had travelled down the main street, that he should ask the driver to halt and then go and report the murder to the local police with the suggestion that they telephone ahead to alert the authorities in Fort Etienne. Then he decided, for several reasons, against following up on this thought. It was, after all, only just after dawn, and the men at the station were hardly likely to be as alert as they would need to be. This would result in endless delays while the local police chief was aroused and made up his mind just how far his jurisdiction went in this particular instance. He might decide to start the investigation himself, there and then, which could mean a holdup of hours, if not days. Also there was no guarantee that there would be a telephone connection to Fort Etienne, because the copper wire used in the system to connect the two cities was a much prized commodity, locally, for making jewelry, with the result that it was frequently cut down at night in lengths of up to a mile. Having been melted, it would reappear in the market later as necklaces and bracelets.

Quarshie scrambled awkwardly out into the gangway and stood up, a massive figure blocking the view through the central part of the windscreen for those sitting further back down the aisle. Then, looking to the right and left at the other passengers as he passed them, he made his way slowly towards the back of the coach.

When he reached the seat occupied by the lawyer, the man held up his hand and caught Quarshie by the elbow. "You're Doctor Quarshie, aren't you?" he asked. And when Quarshie nodded, the lawyer jerked his head in the direction of the corpse and demanded, "So what do you think of that?"

It was an empty-minded question with a completely predictable answer. Quarshie gave it. "Bad," he said, "bad."

"That's what I think myself."

"That's what every educated person should think," the lawyer's companion chipped in.

"It does not concern you professionally, though, eh?" the lawyer wanted to know. "They were suggesting at the stop back there that you are on holiday."

"As a doctor it concerns me," Quarshie told the man, "though there is nothing I could have done, because he was dead when I reached him."

"Ah, but I meant as an investigator. If you got after the murderer, he would not have much hope of getting away with it."

Quarshie shook his head. "The storytellers exaggerate my capabilities."

"Have you failed to find the culprit in any case that you have taken on?"

"People give themselves away rather easily."

"It may seem like that to you, but apparently it does not seem like that to the police. So, are you going to involve yourself in this one?"

Quarshie disliked lying, even in a good cause. He replied, "I am a doctor, and as such I can attend to the sick and wounded without being called upon to do so. When a crime has been committed, that is something else altogether."

Everyone within earshot was listening.

"Who go kill dat man, sah?" The question came from a poorly dressed traveller in a nearby seat. He was holding an open bottle of beer and had another empty one on the seat beside him. "You know who go kill 'um, sah, you go tell me. Den I go kill dis man . . ." He paused, not knowing how to finish his thought. It came to him. "Den I go kill dis man dat go kill dat man."

Quarshie told the lawyer, "It's a matter for the local police, since it happened on Transnigerian soil. Perhaps you will back up the driver when he makes his report, since it is your country too, isn't it?"

"Of course, of course . . . I shall certainly do my duty, and I shall also tell the police that you were on the bus and that if they want results they should get you on the job right away."

For the second time Quarshie shook his head. "That might be

rather undiplomatic," he told the man he was growing to dislike more and more every moment, "even if I could live up to the flattering view you have of me. Now, if you will excuse me, I was on my way to the toilet." And he moved in that direction, thinking that one of the most unpleasant aspects of fame was that it made those who recognised him want to be able to boast afterwards to their friends that they had given him the benefit of their views. Undoubtedly, as he had expected, he had been known to some of the Akhanaians, who might have bragged about him to the Transnigerians, making the same extravagant claims for his capabilities that were being made in the stories that were being circulated about him in the market-places in Akhana.

The toilet compartment, when he entered it, stank abominably, and he understood why so many people had got off the bus and walked away into the bush at the last stop. Nonetheless, he had to stay in there long enough to give substance to the fiction that he had a conventional reason for being in there. Then he returned slowly to his place by the door.

Sitting with his eyes closed, he recalled the rows of passengers as he had seen them. The development of an exceptional ability to memorise what they saw or heard was very common amongst Africans, being a beneficial fallout of illiteracy. For instance, because they were unable to make shopping lists or to read them if others made them, the women developed the ability to memorise the shopping requirements of a dozen other women in the village they lived in. Quarshie could remember his mother setting out for the market in a town twenty-five miles away, her mind stuffed with the requirements of half the other women in the village in which they had lived. Very seldom, when she returned, had she made any mistakes or forgotten to make a requested purchase.

At university, in Canada, Quarshie had worked hard to improve the visual side of this inherited capability to memorise what he was told or what he saw. In the end it had served him well, particularly in physiology and other studies where the ability to reproduce an accurate mental picture of a diagram, or of tissues or other specimens he had examined with a microscope, as well as all kinds of other photomicrographic evidence, had helped him to gain high marks in his examinations.

So, now, in his mind's eye he checked over what he had seen of his fellow passengers and found them to be a nondescript collection. His problem, of course, was that he was looking for a face in a crowd without knowing what distinguishing features it might possess.

Amongst those he had looked at were the professional men who had tried, but failed, to get the bus across the bridge over the Niger. There were several younger men and women who might have been students. There were two or three wealthy-looking elderly women as well as a number of passengers of both sexes whose fares were probably being paid by relatives, because they looked to Quarshie to be too poor to pay for their tickets themselves. Finally, there were several Transnigerians who had probably left their poor subsistence farms in the North and had gone to the Coast to make their fortunes. Whether they had been successful or not was hard to tell, because even though they might have no more money than they could jingle in one pocket, they were all dressed to suggest that they were going home in triumph, rich enough to buy more wives, horses, cattle, land, and everything which gave a man status in his native village. Quarshie knew, however, that this apparent prosperity might be even less than skin deep. Their clothes might not belong to them, but to their "brothers"—the other people of their clan who inhabited with them the visitors' zongo in Port St. Mary.

After considerable thought, Quarshie found that there was not one amongst the whole busload whom he instinctively distrusted or who seemed to be embarrassed by his survey.

His intuition, he thought, was not acute enough, and then he laughed at himself for considering that it might be. And yet, he consoled himself, those who scorned what people called intuition did so at their own peril. As a sixth sense, or something like it, it was a force to be contended with and one which Africans accepted more readily than white Westerners. When it could be controlled, concentrated and ordered, like light beamed through a laser, he speculated, it would be a greater source of power, for better or worse, than most of the others which men have developed so far. The world is coming to it, he thought, and Africans will have much to contribute when someone finally starts to pour the kind of money into research in the subject that will be needed to bring the powers to light so that they can be examined.

Which has not happened yet, he reminded himself.

So the only man on the bus who knew, at that moment, who had committed the murder was the killer himself.

He opened his eyes and saw that, at last, after little more than sixteen hours, the bus was entering the outskirts of Fort Etienne, and he knew from past experience that this would normally be the noisiest part of the trip because the bus driver had inherited something of the spirit of the one-time European coachmen who used to announce their arrival at their destination with a trumpeter constantly blowing a post horn. In the case of the ex-Greyhound bus, it was twin electric horns which the driver used to inform everyone of the triumphant ending of another hazardous run. Usually, too, the crowds waved to the driver, and he waved back with one dignified, white-gloved hand, like royalty accepting the plaudits of their subjects. Today, unhappily, the coach carried a dead man, and the horns, as was proper to the occasion, were only sounded—and then in a muted way—to clear a passage for the bus through the sheep, goats, cattle, head-loaded market-going women, and men on horses and bicycles.

As they were crossing the bridge over the Niger—the river coiled back on itself many times in its more than two-thousand-mile journey to the sea—Quarshie was jolted by an unhappy memory.

The dead man had said that his wife was going to meet him. She would be at the terminus, and he, Quarshie, was going to have to intercept her and break the terrible news to her. It was an unavoidable duty that only he could carry out, because only he knew that she would be meeting the bus.

Combined with the man's death, the fulfillment of this duty was going to make the early hours of this day amongst the hardest that he had ever experienced. It was also a most unhappy overture to an assignment that he had, from the beginning, been very reluctant to accept. For a moment he almost regretted his close relationship with the old Frenchman. Then his better judgement told him that it was ridiculous to blame the actions of fate on any human being, and he steeled himself wearily to do the best he could for the unknowing widow.

If he had had complete foreknowledge of everything which lay ahead of him during the next few weeks, all the anxiety and trouble that was waiting for him, it is doubtful that he would have stayed on the bus until it arrived. Instead, he would have asked the driver to let him off. Then he would have taken the next form of transport, be it bus, taxi, truck or donkey, back to Port St. Mary. He might even have walked.

TWO

Count not for whom the bell tolls, it tolls for thee. No matter how much of a saint or a swine you are.

It was awful. She screamed and went terribly red in the face. I expected her to collapse.

Quarshie was part of the way into a diary he was keeping for his wife. She had been unable to accompany him to Transniger because she was representing Akhana at a conference on family planning in Dakar.

She had not wanted to go. She had said that even though she was a practicing midwife she was not the right person to talk about birth control, because she had never borne a child. She had also complained that it meant leaving the Quarshies' adopted son, Arimi, with relatives.

Quarshie had been firm. He had told her that she must not allow her interests to become too narrow. To which she had replied stormily by asking what kind of African he thought he was to suggest that her interests were too narrow when they were traditional to the extent that she only had time in her life for her husband, her son and her work. Africa has to move out of the past if it is to survive in the modern world, Quarshie had told her; therefore, as an educated and enlightened woman it was up to her to help to lead her people in the right direction.

He knew that the truth was that she found it shameful to have to admit that she had no children of her own, that she was shy and that she disliked having to mix with unfamiliar people in unfamiliar surroundings. She was at home with patients in hospitals and clinics, and ill-at-ease surrounded by people with academic degrees. This made her argumentative and aggressive, and she did not like to have to confront this side of her nature.

It had been a Sunday and their discussion had gone on all day until the French Ambassador had arrived unexpectedly on their doorstep.

He had at once been made party to their difference of opinion and had taken the wind out of Mrs. Quarshie's sails when he had told her that she had been invited to the conference on his recommendation.

"It is sad to say it," he had told her, "but most of the people who are going to this affair are *conférencières professionelles, tu sait, madame?* They go from one such business to another. So, if the *conférence* is to 'ave any kind of *vitalité,* we must 'ave some people there who will speak the truth from the heart."

Then, having scored that point, the Ambassador had gone straight on to make the next one.

"But to get you a nice trip to Dakar, *ma chère madame,* was not my real reason for coming here this evening. Since, of course, you will go . . . it makes it easier for me to ask the favour I wish of your big 'usband. For, you understand, if you are not here he will not need to be here either. Is that not good *logique?* So you will not mind, I am sure, that I borrow Quarshie for a little while. It will only be for a few days, you know?" And before she could protest, he had whisked the Doctor off to the Embassy to "fill him in" on the details of the job he wanted him to do.

It was a subject he tackled in a grimly serious tone of voice.

"There is only one way it all makes sense," he had said after telling Quarshie about the three whites who had been murdered with a garrotte. "It must be someone with an *animosité* against the white man. There is no connection between these men who are *étranglé.* And always it is in the same way with the garrotte. My friend, the *Général,* is a very good man. I expect he is the only politician in the world who is too honest to be in politics. I have to say that he is truly the father of his country. I have known him for almost all my career. We are like brothers and I am proud to say it."

So it followed that Mrs. Quarshie had gone one way, tearfully, saying that she knew she was going to be sick on the aeroplane, and Quarshie had gone the other way after she had made him promise to keep a truthful and complete diary of everything which happened while he was away in the North.

To keep his promise and despite the fact that the twenty-four hours he had to describe had been almost unbearably trying, Quarshie had left his bed before dawn and was now labouring over a schoolboy's exercise book, his gold pencil always lagging far behind his thoughts and memories.

Poor woman, he wrote. *She cried. She swore. I don't think she knew what she was doing. She said, "I told him over and over again that he ought to retire and go home. But he kept saying, 'They need me here, they need me here.' They needed him so badly they had to kill him. Why? Why, when he only lived to do good?"*

That was the beginning of a terrible day.

And the fool Mamadou, the local official who is supposed to be helping me, was late.

He excused himself by saying that his Imam delayed him when he went to get a blessing on our efforts. And he brought a newspaper which he showed me with great pride. It had a long story in it about my pending arrival, who I was, what I had done, how lucky Trans-niger is to have the services of such a brilliant man at this critical moment in its history, and so on and so on.

The paper, Mamadou explained, is owned by his uncle.

The General's Chef de Cabinet is another of Mamadou's uncles.

So, it seems, is the Chief Commissioner of Police.

If I am lucky and do not beat this elegant and aristocratic young man after he has turned up late for some other vital function, or because he has made some other terrible blunder like getting all that nonsense about me printed in the press, I shall at least have someone who can direct me to all the people who matter . . . because he is obviously related to them all.

Now back to the beginning so that I can set my day down in order.

The man had been murdered on the bus. I have told you that already. And his wife was to meet him at the bus station where Mamadou was also supposed to be waiting for me, but wasn't.

I was left with the dead man, his wife and the bus driver.

All the passengers just walked away—the lawyer who was going to do his duty, and all of them, because there was no one to stop them or to question them.

I got a taxi and took my two live companions and the dead one to the police station.

That in itself was quite an experience.

Why not leave the corpse in the bus and send the driver to fetch the police? Because the passengers had spread the word that there was a dead white man on the coach and something like a football crowd was beginning to form around us. The woman would not be parted from her husband and I couldn't leave them alone. Also, I was afraid that the bus driver would not be believed by the police. So I sent him for a taxi.

Partial rigor mortis had stiffened the man in something like a sitting position, so we carried him, shaped like that, through the crowd to the back seat of the taxi. I sat on one side of the body, and his wife sat on the other. His skin was already pale and waxy, and his eyes terribly bloodshot because a lot of blood vessels had broken in them. I think his wife was trying all the time not to look at him, but her head kept turning back in his direction. The bus driver sat in the front seat, beside the owner of the taxi, still wearing his white gloves.

At the police station we carried the dead man in, the bus driver and I, and sat him in one corner, on the floor, against the wall.

Gruesome is the word, I think, for the whole proceeding, and it was obviously a nightmare for the man's wife.

The sergeant on duty did not want to hear anything about the case. He was the one who found the victim of the last garrotting, and it had complicated his life and duties beyond all imagination. The Superintendent would take my report, he told me.

The dead man's wife had sunk right down to the bottom. She had nothing to say and no more tears to cry.

I told the sergeant that somebody was supposed to be meeting me.

"Yessah," he replied, "Mamadou Jayallo, sah."

I then told him to take care of the corpus delicti until the Superintendent arrived, and to send for another taxi so that I could take the woman to her house. I also told him that I would come right back to talk with his superior and that he should send someone to look for Mamadou.

When we arrived at her bungalow the woman was so dispirited that she did exactly what I told her. There was a special decoration on the table with a bottle of whisky and a package with a blue bow on it. There was also a card with "Welcome home, darling" and "Happy Birthday" on it.

I thought that the agony she was suffering was going to kill her.

She said, in a listless way, "It's all a bit pointless, isn't it, Doctor? Rotten people are allowed to live and good ones get killed. Nothing makes sense. I am sure you are a good man like he was, but will that make any difference to what happens to you? 'Count not for whom the bell tolls, it tolls for thee.' No matter how much of a swine or a saint you are. Why do we bother to keep ourselves alive?" She held out her hand. "Good-bye," she told me. "Be careful. Don't throw away your life after his, trying to catch the fiend who did it. No, don't say anything. Just go quietly, please . . . and thank you for your help." She wore her grey hair in a bun at the back of her head, and it had slipped out of the comb and was hanging untidily onto her shoulder, but she did not notice it.

She had learned who I was and why I was in Fort Etienne from the conversation I had had with the sergeant at the police station.

I went back to see the Superintendent and to find Mamadou waiting, clutching his newspaper, which was to be a big surprise especially prepared for my arrival.

The Superintendent was quick and efficient, and I was soon alone with my new assistant.

Mamadou is very thin, though he showed later, when we had some food together, that he could eat enough to fill three normal men. Like almost all the Muslims here, he surrounds himself with many folds of white cloth and wears a little round, embroidered hat.

I felt sorry for him in a way. He had wanted to make a good impression on me, and everything he had done had gone wrong. Worst of all, I think, was the fact that I was angry about the piece he had had printed in the paper about me. He had taken a great deal of trouble with it and had evidently had his mental image of me all wrong. I am sure the blessing he asked for from Allah included me, too.

He looks a bit like one of those carvings of gazelles you see everywhere up here. He has the same long face, long upper lip and huge eyes. I learned later from the General that he is a poet and a writer.

That was the best thing that happened to me all day . . . my visit to the old man. I will write more about it in a moment.

The kind of relationship Mamadou seems to be trying to establish with me is explained by the local word barshun'a.

It describes an exaggerated form of a tradition we also have in my village. In fact, almost all village Africans have it, and it is only you city-born and -bred people who have abandoned it.

Barshun'a is a discipline-respect relationship between an older and a younger man. It has as an opposite, burunga, which is a shame-avoidance relationship. Both are still strictly observed here and relate to another which you might call a "father of the house" cult. In this case, "father" can mean the head of a business or anyone whose position makes him responsible for the well-being of others. Barshun'a is what is owed to these "fathers" by their dependents, who all try very *hard to get themselves accepted as members of a community in which there is someone in a "father of the house" position. This means behaving like a son and trying to get the father to accept this relationship. One of the principal ways of securing oneself in that position is to get the father to permit the son to perform some service for him.*

This was the technique, I think, Mamadou was trying to work on me with his newspaper article. If I accept him as a member of my household—house son, they call it—it carries serious obligations on both sides. He must show himself to be subdued, self-controlled and obedient to certain traditional rules of behaviour in his relationship with me. While I must give him protection, security, status, and take his side in any dispute he gets into. I explain all this because nowhere that I have been are these patterns of behaviour as strictly enforced as they are here. I am telling you about them, also, so that you will see a few of the difficulties which lie ahead because this young man, Mamadou, is extremely well-connected, and if I don't play his game I could have difficulties with some very important people.

What it all amounts to is that if this relationship develops the way Mamadou wants it to—and given all the other circumstances, I don't see how I can avoid accepting him on these principles—I will have got myself another son who appears, on first sight, to be wayward, impulsive, spoilt and temperamental, as well as a fanatical Muslim. On the credit side, so far, I think he is intelligent, in an artistic sort of a way, sensitive, and if he accepts his side of the contract as totally as he, undoubtedly, expects me to accept mine, then I shall have a follower who will be loyal to me to the last breath in his body.

At the point where I freed myself of the Superintendent and started to get acquainted with Mamadou, it was about half past ten and I was tired, I had not washed properly for about twenty-four hours, and he told me we had an appointment to see the General in fifteen minutes! The police allowed me to wash and put on a clean suit, the new one I bought in Senegal the last time I was there, in the best-scrubbed wash place I have ever found anywhere. This improved my opinion of the sergeant who is in charge of the station.

We took a taxi to the Residence.

This is a strange country. Though few people know it, it is one of the few in the world where both English and French are accepted as official languages. Mamadou's uncle, whom we would call the Presi-

dent's Permanent Secretary, prefers to be known as the Chef de Cabinet, and both he and the General have French as their first language.

The Residence is also unusual for a West African state, because it is not heavily guarded by the military and has only regular police on duty at the main gate.

Mamadou told me that the General holds regular hours every day, in the old style, when the people of the country can visit him and discuss their problems with him personally. Nor is there any screening process involved. They line up in order of arrival and he takes them in turn. Those he does not see keep their place in the queue, and though they may have to wait a day or two, they all see him eventually. The only security precaution which is enforced is that all his visitors are searched for weapons in the anteroom before they go in to talk with him, and the only restriction, unless he personally waives the rule, is that they only get ten minutes each to explain their problem or to tell him whatever it is they have on their minds.

A more extreme contrast in personalities than exists between the Head of State and his Chef de Cabinet would be hard to find.

The General is the personification of the ideal, traditional African chief. As the French Ambassador had told me, he is "the father of his country," wise, sincere, kindly by instinct, prepared to listen to his petitioners and to believe in their honesty of purpose. At least that is the impression he gives.

The Chef de Cabinet is cynical, cautious and highly intellectual. My suspicion is that he makes quick, unromantic judgements of those who pass through his hands on the way to see the General and he passes his views on to him, thus allowing the old man to be on his guard without ever seeming to be suspicious.

They make a perfect combination and are probably the reason that, until now, this very poor country is one of the most peaceful and best-governed in West Africa. It is all the more poisonous, therefore, for them to find themselves the centre of the kind of attention these murders are causing.

I think I established a good understanding with both of them from my first meeting. The thing they share is integrity of purpose. They want the country to be well-governed, from the Chef de Cabinet's point of view, despite the usual corruption, nepotism and greed, while the General pities his people for their weaknesses and wants to help them to overcome them.

Physically they are different, too.

The Chef de Cabinet is more Arab, or Fulani, sharp-featured, wiry and given to gesticulation.

The General, on the other hand—well, I might look something like he does when I get to his age. He is deliberate in the way he speaks, slow in response, as though he is weighing every word he says, and generally he is more like we people of the coast both in appearance and manner.

They both spoke French with me and they both knew, already, about the murder on the bus.

Their reactions were perhaps typical of their characters.

"So, you come to solve the mystery of sudden death, and to prove that you are well-acquainted with it you bring it with you." That was the flippant way the Chef de Cabinet greeted me.

"How tragic for the widow and how disturbing it must have been for you," was the way the General reacted.

The Chef de Cabinet restrained Mamadou's move to join me when I went in to see the General.

The old man has a stubble of grey hair on his head and a very prominent gold tooth, and he was wearing a suit exactly like mine. His expression was calm and welcoming, and he got up from an armchair near a big window to greet me. Beyond the window there is a distant view of the Niger and a ragged hillside which looks like a bony old brown dog lying with its back towards the Residence. It is hot out there, but not as hot as it will be in a couple of months. Somebody told me they recorded a temperature of one hundred and thirty degrees in the shade up here last year. It is surprising to see how much water there still is in the river.

The General waved me to another comfortable chair, so that we were both sitting half facing the window and half facing each other. Without any opening formalities he spoke directly of what was on his mind, as if we had been acquainted for a long time.

"Which is the worst to witness, Doctor, the end of a life brought about by some terrible disease, or the victim of a murder?"

The words were unexpected and I had no ready answer.

I replied, "I don't know, sir. The death of a patient can sometimes be a very personal defeat, so I suppose one feels it the worst. Neither kind of death comes really as a shock or a surprise to me any more."

"You speak as a man of much experience."

"Enough, sir, to suggest that we make much too much fuss about death. Nothing in the world is more commonplace or happens more often."

"Yet you try to catch murderers and take a good many risks to do it."

"Because any form of killing of men by other men causes fear and mistrust and therefore misery for the living."

"You are not a violent man, yourself, Doctor?"

"I try not to be."

He nodded, "How much have you been told about the murders of whites that have been happening here?"

"A little, but I would like to have your opinions about them, too, sir."

"Two of the dead men I knew quite well. Like your Catholic relief-agency man, there seems to have been no possible motive for anyone to want to kill either of them. One of them was the son of an old friend of mine in France—he was a stagiaire at the Embassy. He asked to complete his training here because I had visited his family's house at Honfleur, had met him as a schoolboy and had liked him. He was a warmhearted, intelligent youth who could not possibly have harmed anybody." The old man looked troubled as he was speaking. "The only possible thing against him is that I . . . is that I treated him as if he were my own son. He had a parrot called Pompidou in a big cage in a compound in his quarters. One night he went out because, as a joke, he was trying to teach it to sing that song about John Brown's body in English, but with a French accent. When he did not come back after about an hour, the other stagiaire, who shared the accommodation with him, went out to look for him and found him dead, murdered. His parents have been very understanding, but it was—how can you believe this? but it is true—as much of a loss to me as it was to them. I have told you of this case first, because it is the only one in which you could say that I am personally involved."

The General sat gazing out of the window seeing things he did not want to tell me about, and it was a long time before he spoke again. Then he said, "Number two—you see they are not people any more, they are just numbers—number two was a Swiss employed by UNESCO as the director of their local Alphabetisation programme. Ninety-four per cent of our people are illiterate. The man was an enthusiast and a rebel. He was always inventing new ways to try to teach people—if the conventional way did not work he would devise another. He never taught in classes but worked with groups, out on their farms with them, making them laugh, and then with their help translating the joke into Mussi, or whatever their language was, and *writing it down. He painted the names of all the tools they used on the tools themselves—in fact, he labelled everything they lived with and hung cards round their necks with their names printed on them. He never used a book until they could read and write. No man who has taught our people has ever been as successful as he was, and I think everybody who had anything to do with him loved him. Then he was killed as he was walking back to his hut one evening from the local chief's hut. If it had not been for the fact that a garrotte was used to murder him, we might, I suppose, have thought that it was one of the local people who did it. The local chief swore that there was nobody who would have wished to see the man dead; in fact, there were several who had told the chief that they would have given their lives to save his.*

"So those are the two men I knew personally." The General got up and went to his desk and came back with a file which he handed to me.

"If after you have read this you need more information, ask anyone whom you think might be able to give it to you. The third victim is listed in there, and I don't even know what he looked like.

"He was a Russian working for their Cultural Mission here. Of course he was a member of the KGB. They really think we are childish, you know, that we cannot recognise monkey business when we see it. The man was keeping an eye on an American who sells arms as well as heavy-duty road-building and bridging equipment. Everyone around the Russian—his houseboy, the cleaner who worked at the Cultural Mission, the man who drove his car—were playing 'no-savvy' boys, and they were all reporting directly to my Chef de Cabinet. Another of our anti-espionage people was working as his gardener, and he it was who found the man's body face down in a bed of canna lilies." He paused before adding,

"Now, there is your man who was killed on the bus. It is all so random.

"Our police are not fools. They have asked thousands of questions of hundreds of people, but no one who might be seen as suspicious has ever been reported anywhere in the neighbourhood of anyplace where these people were killed. All the garrottes are identical. However, there are no other clues . . . footmarks in the loose dust, some indications which suggest that perhaps there may have been a car in the vicinity, but no witnesses, nothing stolen, no gossip. The killers are as invisible as the wind and seem to come and go just as easily as it does.

"Doctor, this is terribly serious for our country because we need the aid we get from Europe and the U.S.A. more than most of the countries here. We had rain last season for the first time in three years, but still fifty thousand of our people will die from the effect of the previous years of drought through cumulative malnutrition which makes them susceptible to such diseases as measles, meningitis, pneumonia and endemic diarrhea. So we have to stop this maniac, or these maniacs, who are not just killing the whites but are helping to kill our people too by turning those who want to help us against us.

"And then, there is the fact that they killed my friend's son. When my people suffer because of the activities of evil men, it is my friends they are injuring. When they come closer and injure those who are my intimates, they injure me personally. That is why I wanted to see you and speak with you. I want to make you an intimate and therefore intimately involved in my affairs."

I left the Residence afterwards with a hot coal of hatred burning in my belly. It was fuelled and fired by men who wantonly destroy in others that small spark of magic we have been unable to define except by calling it life. To make the punishment fit the crime, I would take away from them all those senses which put us above an earthworm but leave them with the everlasting ache that would tell them what they had lost.

My anger with them has its root, of course, in the fact that they have aroused my feelings to the point of making me vindictive. Yesterday it was for what they did to that wretched widow. Today, it is for what they have done and are doing to all the people in this country. There are no words to express my feelings.

Poor Mamadou, he cannot comprehend what is going wrong and accept the possibility that it is I who am out of phase with everything and that he is not to blame.

He had booked me into the local Intercontinental Hotel and I refused to stay there. I do not want a lot of rich expatriates around me fussing about the food and the service and treating me as some kind of freak because I can understand their culture. They behave like visitors at a zoo and they make me sick.

So Mamadou had to go and cancel my room while I sat and glowered in the taxi outside.

I told him I wanted to stay at the Hotel Buffet de la Gare, where I once stayed when I was first in government practice just over the frontier and all these countries were still colonies. After that I sent Mamadou home and told him not to worry, that I shall be easier to work with after I have had a good night's rest.

I must have slept for two or three hours and then I went out for a walk to see if I could find myself, because instead of there being some sort of order in my mind, everything was scrambled.

All I found were lots of other people, and they all looked at me as if I were a more or less ordinary human being. On that point I was one up on them because I knew I was not, and I doubted whether I would be again until this business is over. Not only my mind but my feelings are all out of register. I can't seem to get them tuned in properly. Obviously I am not confronted with anything like any of the murder cases I have encountered to date. The indications are, so far, that someone is fighting a private war and his methods and motivations are not in any way similar to those I, or the police, have dealt with before. And all this quite apart from the fact that murder up here is a very rare occurrence.

I have always, in my other efforts to find murderers, been able to believe that the killers had something more or less rational to gain from their efforts—financial profit, for instance, or power, or personal revenge. In this instance, as the French Ambassador suggested at the very beginning, the only motive has to be something which, without any sense of selection, includes all the white people. If this is true, the massacre can go on for as long as there are any white people to kill, and there is no way of knowing where the killer will strike next.

With that negative thought in my mind I went back to the hotel.

As the name suggests, it is part of a railway station, the terminus of a line which starts in Miwiville, on the coast, and meanders up to Fort Etienne like a disorientated snake.

The railway and the hotel were built many years ago by French railway engineers. The material they had to use in the construction of the railway was the same that they used to build the hotel, the framework made of the massive steel girders they use to build bridges. They bolted a square, three-story frame of these together, put down a double layer of massive planks for floors—one lot running north and south, the other east and west—and filled in the framework of beams with steel plate and bricks. Perhaps the idea was to use the place for a last-ditch stand in case the natives got restless. Whatever their intentions, it must be one of the strongest buildings in the world and the only one with every room an exact cube. Later they stuck wooden verandahs onto the back and the front, three stories high.

In the angle between the side of the hotel and the big driveway which leads up to the station, there is a planting of trees which look like eucalyptus, only they are taller and thicker. Amongst the trees there is an open-air dance floor with a seven-piece band . . . that is, if you call a singer a "piece," which he certainly is in this instance.

There are tables around the dance floor, and I sat at one and ordered a beer.

After the fourth bottle I began to think I was finding myself. That means I was beginning to take a normal interest in my surroundings.

The music is mostly Kinshasha style, with a few high-lifes and Afro-South American numbers. Five of the band belong to the rhythm section, and the melodies are carried by the trumpeter or the singer, either as solos, or together in unison or harmony. I enjoyed it because it worked on my mind like an eraser.

Then I got intrigued with the singer.

He is an albino and he is the fount of the music. The trumpeter can hit a sour note occasionally or blur a phrase. The singer, on the other hand, with the whole of his being is the note, or the words; he is tuned exactly to the subtleties of inflection, the rhythmic breaks, changes of key, the beat, everything, and he swings his phrases with the assurance of the great black singers of American jazz. His body is part of the act, too, moving with or against the beat, getting something from it and giving something to it.

When they were having a rest and someone in a booth beside the band was playing records, I sent my waiter over to the albino with a note telling him I would like to buy him a drink. By then I was on my fifth or sixth beer, and a little detail slipped my mind. I signed my name, forgetting that Mamadou had had it printed all over one of the inside pages of the Morning Star.

It was something which had not escaped the attention of the albino.

He came over at once and brought one of the guitarists with him.

As I called for more beer, the young man told the guitarist in French—one of the things Mamadou's article had not said was that I speak French—"We are about to drink in distinguished company, Justin." And to me he said, "It was très gentil of you, sir, to say that you like our music."

In French I told him, "Your 'distinguished company' did not say *that he enjoyed your music, though I do. What I said was that I enjoyed your singing very much indeed."*

He was looking at me out of those strange albino eyes with peculiar intensity. "Excuse me, sir, I did not know that you spoke French. You are the *Doctor Quarshie, aren't you?"*

"Some people have called me that."

"Then you are a very influential man, sir. You have met our President and you are a friend of the President of Akhana."

"I don't know how influential I am—that is, how much attention important people give to what I tell them—but I have met your President, and Colonel Jedawi, my President, allows me to visit him occasionally."

"My friend and I would like to sing and play for you, sir, so that you can tell your important friends how good we are, like you told me just now."

The alcohol was affecting me a little bit and I told myself . . . ah, another case of barshun'a.

But still I was interested, and it was not just in his singing.

Ginger-coloured hair, skin as white as flour but speckled with brown blotches, weak, pinkish eyes, typically African features, thick lips, nose with a broad, flat bridge and wide nostrils, and something very unusual which went beyond his voice and his music. The interest was something he sensed, too, because there was a puzzled gleam in his eyes which suggested to me that we must talk privately together somewhere. What is the mystery? There is some meaning this meeting holds that neither of us can touch. Something out in limbo which I am sure is very important.

"We'll talk some more about it later," I told him. "I have to hear you sing a lot more first, and we have to get better acquainted."

It was a suggestion which clearly met his approval. "Yes, sir," he said, "I shall have to go back and sing in a minute. Shall I come and talk with you some other time?"

"When do you start here at night?"

"At half past nine."

"I will try to be here tomorrow at half past eight. Look out for me."

"Yes, sir."

Then he went back to sing. It must have been almost dawn before he stopped. Every time I woke up—which was often because they were shunting and making up freight trains all night with a noisy diesel locomotive, and there was an open-air movie close enough for me to hear people coughing in the audience, gun fights, the sirens of police cars and the screams of frightened women, and it must have run until two o'clock in the morning—every time I woke up I could still hear him singing, with the rhythm section pounding the beat behind him.

Prudence, I am full of anxiety. Do you remember your cousin Peter telling us what it feels like to be in the West Indies before a hurricane hits? The same feeling of menace is in the atmosphere here. And I feel so helpless. There is nothing I can do until I can get something to work with, something that will enable me to build some kind of picture of what is going on. But how can I do that when I don't know where to begin?

THREE

. . . chastisement with fire awaiteth them.

I am tired after another period of fumbling for facts, another terrible event, and a strange evening spent with the albino, Michel N'Dama. Quarshie was back with his diary. *At last the day is ending. There were moments when I thought it was going to last forever.*

With Mamadou trailing languidly and reluctantly behind me, I visited all those who worked with, or for, all the victims. I also questioned the police whose reports I had been shown, and I found what I had been told I would find.

Nothing.

That took up most of my day from half past seven until four. It was very hot. Only Mamadou, dressed in all his sheets of white cloth, looked cool.

There is something approaching panic developing amongst the expatriates here. Several of them are insisting on police protection, others are putting day watchmen on their houses as well as having them around at night. In some cases they have two of them on together. One white man has even brought a time clock back from the mill where he works, and the nightwatchmen have to punch it every half hour.

At four o'clock we received a telephone call and Mamadou told me that his uncle, the newspaper editor, would like to see me. I could tell that he expected me to be angry, because he was quick to tell me that the man wanted to discuss something which had been sent to him that I might consider evidence.

Looking at him then, I decided that Mamadou might have qualities which I have overlooked. Both his uncles, the Chef de Cabinet and the newspaper editor, are intelligent men of superior competence. The same is true of the Chief of Police.

The newspaper editor's name is Alhaji Baba Dababa. He is small and dynamic. All his movements are quick and darting, like a little gecko. When he speaks, his words seem to be pushing each other out of his mouth in their hurry to get spoken.

The paper he edits is printed in English and French.

"I hope I have not brought you here on a wild-goose chase, Doctor," he told me. "I am afraid to offer what I have here to the police. They might laugh at me. Nonetheless, I am pretty certain that it is connected with this terrible business and that it will help an intuitive man like you. I discovered this envelope earlier this afternoon quite by accident in the drawer of my secretary's desk. She had probably dismissed the contents as rubbish sent by some crank. We get a lot of this stuff, considering how many of our people are illiterate. Most of those who can hold a pen must spend their time writing to me. My secretary has had a death in her family, so she has had to travel to her village for a few days. The date on which we received each of these items was always a day or two before one of the atrocities you are investigating was committed. I have put the notes in the order in which we received them. Here is the first one."

The verse he gave me was written on a piece of lined paper which looked as if it had been torn out of a schoolboy's exercise book. It was carefully printed in block letters.

It read:

Bear in mind
that death is a drum
beating forever
till the last worms come
to answer its call
till the last stars fall
until the last atom of all
until time is lost
and there is no air
and space itself
is nothing nowhere.

"The other pieces are quite different," Dababa told me.

Mamadou took the piece of paper away from me and read the poem. He had the look of a man standing on a scaffold with a rope around his neck waiting for the executioner.

His uncle said, "Here it comes," and pointing at Mamadou, he added, "the original memory man himself."

Mamadou said, "Hughes, Langston. Selected Poems. 1959."

"That's clever of you," I told him.

In a rather superior way he said, "I am a poet. I must read the works of other poets."

"Langston Hughes was, or is, an Afro-American?"

"Was. Which means nothing," Mamadou replied. "He is widely read here, and his works are studied in the last year at the English language secondary schools." He was already ahead of the thought, which I had not expressed, that there might be some link to an Afro-American writer of crank letters. So that piece of intuition was knocked off the score sheet. However, Mamadou had revealed the first of his personal skills which would finally prove him to be the best assistant, aside from yourself, Prudence, I have ever had.

"Here is the next one." Dababa gave me another sheet of paper from a school exercise book. "It came just before the Swiss literacy expert was murdered."

I read it aloud.

"He it is who caused the unbelievers among the people of the Book to leave their homes and join those who had gone away already. Ye did not think that they would leave their homes: and they for their part thought that their defences would protect them against God: but God came upon them from an unexpected direction and with the victorious believers caused them to fear so mightily that they demolished their own houses. Those who can understand this should profit by this thing they have seen.

"And were it not that God had determined that they should go into exile, surely in this world He would have chastised them: however, in the world to come, chastisement with fire awaiteth them."

I gave Mamadou a questioning look and he responded immediately. "Easy," he said. "It is a translation of the Koran. Sura fifty-nine. It speaks of the Jews of Nodire who had broken a treaty that they had made with Muhammad."

"Was the Swiss literacy man a Jew?" I asked. His wife had gone back to Switzerland, so I had only been able to talk with the household servants and to read the police file.

"I don't know," Mamadou replied, "but the Director of Education should have that information in his files. I will telephone him."

"Is he also an uncle of yours?" I asked.

My intended humour missed the mark altogether. Solemnly Mamadou replied, "No. But he is of my mother's people, from the same village."

While he put through his phone call I looked at the next text. They were all written in the same hand and on the same kind of paper.

It read: "Deceit is his middle name and the middle name of all his brothers. His people pretend equality but the strength of the majority nonetheless supports the few, and the first remain first and the last, last. Their flag is the colour of blood and they are blind to the fact that it is their own blood that it celebrates, the blood of those who refuse to say 'yes' and persist in answering 'no' to those who rule them. They will cheat those who have the biggest name for cheating and lie more subtly than any other liars . . . and those who will be a friend to them will become their slaves."

"Oracular," I told Dababa. "This is the one which preceded the death of the Russian, right?" The editor nodded.

"Then it is not too difficult to see who the writer was talking about, given that one knows the victim."

"He was a Jew, sir," Mamadou reported as he hung up the telephone. He opened his mouth to say something else, but closed it again as the instrument beside him shrilled suddenly.

"Yes. Yes," he said into the mouthpiece. "What?" It was hard to tell whether his expression showed shock or incredulity. He shook his head and his long face seemed to grow longer. He gave the telephone to me.

The voice on the other end said, "Hullo."

"Hullo," I replied, "Doctor Quarshie here."

"This is the Chief Superintendent of Police, Doctor. There has been another killing. A ten-year-old Dutch girl."

I did not have anything to say.

"Did you hear me, Doctor?"

"Yes. Have you moved the body yet?"

"The parents did."

"What is the address, please?"

He told me and I thanked him and hung up.

I gave Mamadou the address and offered the editor my hand.

Dababa asked if I would mind if he came along with us to watch the way I worked. I withdrew my hand and asked, "On what? The child is dead. This murder will not tell me any more than the last one did. Wait. Was there a warning issued by this crank mail artist for his latest terrorist attack?" Because that is what the killing is all about. It has to be.

"There are five of them," Dababa replied.

I picked them all up from the desk where I had dropped them. Mamadou and I left, and the editor followed in another car.

On the way I read the last two.

The first was in doggerel.

It read:

> *"The British came.*
> *The British went.*
> *Now we ask to have the rent.*
> *And everyday*
> *They smile and tell us, 'Go away.'*
>
> *Beside their thefts*
> *Our blood they spent*
> *And make no sign that they repent.*
> *For this I say*
> *We will repay*
> *With an eye for an eye like their Bible say."*

The "Old Coaster" apparently died for the sins of others. Poor man. Unhappy woman.

And the child?

The note was the shortest of them all.

It read: "None will escape the executioner. For none are born innocent. They all carry in their veins the germ of race discrimination and the false pride of being sheathed in a white skin."

More than anything else, the parents of the child were bewildered.

"Why?" the Dutch woman asked me. "Why her?"

There are several dozen white children in Fort Etienne.

"Why her?"

Why the child in the city who, out of thousands, gets run down by an automobile? I want to reply, but of course I cannot.

"She was such a nice little girl," one of the houseboys offers unasked.

The father said, "If I could only get my hands on the man who did it."

He looked wildly at me and then at Mamadou, as if he expected us to lead him to the murderer.

"That child was innocent. Only a madman could think that he

can bring something constructive out of destroying the innocent. This is madness. The world is mad. I am mad." He spoke English with an accent.

I gave the woman a sedative. I could do nothing for the man. He would not take anything.

"Why should I try for myself to make the pain less? That would be making myself to be a traitor to her. Like . . . like cutting my own arm off from my body because it is hurting me."

We left and went to drink some tea with Dababa, very sweet, flavoured with mint, in tiny cups. There are Muslims who openly drink beer, but Dababa and Mamadou are not amongst them.

The editor was shaken. He said, "I keep thinking about how I would feel if my daughter had been killed like that. I would want to kill those who did it, just like her father did. If I was white and I could be sure the murderer was black, I would pin a judgement of guilty on the whole black race."

I did not say so but I thought that the murderer had something just like that in his mind. But if he wants to warn people, why does he wrap up his cautionary notes in almost undecipherable riddles? Unless it is all part of a campaign to create terror. But with what objective?

"I don't think you can have learned much about the way I work," I told Dababa, to break the feeling of gloom which surrounded us.

"Were you working? I suspect that is all part of the trick. You make people think that you are not working. But no matter how tense the drama, I am certain you keep all the pores of your skin open all the time. Shall I prove it to you? Don't forget that your profession is a bit like mine, and I was watching you."

Mamadou woke up and looked backwards and forwards between us, his patron *and his uncle.*

"You can try."

"Will you be honest with me? Give me honest answers to all my questions?"

"Only if you promise not to print any of them in your paper."

He sighed and said, "Very well."

"All right. Go ahead."

"What was the colour of the woman's dress?"

"It had several colours on a white background. Green, ash-blue and red made up in a pattern of flowers."

"Was she wearing a ring?"

"Two, both on the same finger."

"Could you give me any feature that could be used to identify the man?"

"Physical?" Dababa nodded.

"He had a small mole on his neck just below his right ear."

"What about the impression he made on you with his . . . it came close to hysteria, didn't it?"

"He was giving in to it."

"Why?"

"Probably because, in spite of himself, he had to make a dramatic scene."

"And his wife?"

"Stunned. Much more affected than he was."

"What about the victim? What will remain in your memory about her?"

"The straw and sticks in her hair. She had lost a ribbon off one of those little tufts of hair she had sticking out from the side of her head. Also, she had torn some of her fingernails down to the quick. There was very little bleeding, so she must have torn them, just before she died, on the garrotte."

I asked Mamadou what had come into his mind when he saw the child.

He replied,

> *"He is God alone*
> *God the eternal*
> *He begetteth not and he is not begotten:*
> *And there is none like him."*

"Why?" I asked.

"When you see the evil that men can do, you have to believe that there is some power purer and greater than theirs."

His uncle said, "I told you that working with the Doctor would be more than just an academic exercise."

A comment which Mamadou ignored.

"What do we do now, sir?" he asked me.

"I think, therefore I am," I told him. "At this point that has to be my main function. To cogitate and concentrate. But I have a job for you. First, go back and find out if anyone saw that piece of ribbon that was missing from the child's hair. Second, these warning notes which your uncle has been getting suggest that the author is a Muslim who reads and writes English and is trying to get across the

idea that everyone, even children, with a white skin are expendable. So he is educated, anti-white and probably a Muslim. And these murders have to be the work of an adult. Go quietly to every papeterie *and ask if anyone in any of the places which stock them remembers selling this kind of exercise book to an adult. If you are lucky and find one, ask him about the other points, too. Was the man dressed like a Muslim? Did he speak English? And did he say anything to suggest that he might be anti-white? If the thousand-to-one chance comes off, push the odds a little further and find out if they remember what he looked like.*

Dababa grinned and said, "He would not work for me because I told him that his first job as a reporter would be to report on the weekly meeting of the Women's League and to find clients who would buy space for small advertisements. Now, with you, he has to start with the routine stuff in the same way that he would have had to start with me. There are no shortcuts to the top, Mamadou."

The young man shrugged. "The end result of my work in this case, Uncle, might be more . . . useful than reporting on the small squabbles which take place at the Women's League meetings. And it will certainly be more honourable than giving some rascal a chance to persuade other people to buy something useless like Chinese good luck rings, the Great Key to the Wisdom of Solomon, or Gocifuge candles. Doctor Quarshie will find the man who strangled that poor child, and perhaps, when I learn a little more, I shall be able to help him."

His faith in me is embarrassing, his modesty admirable.

I went back to my room at the hotel to spend a little time in concentrated consideration of what I knew so far about these assassinations. My head seemed to be full of that horrid stuff they give children in Canada: alphabet soup.

Presently I heard a discreet knock on my door.

It was Michel N'Dama. He was early.

He apologised and said he knew I was in my room and that, as he had a strong urge to see me, he had felt that he had had to come up.

"How did you know I was in my room?" I enquired.

He shrugged. He just knew. He also knew that he had to come and talk with me because it would be important for both of us.

I was wearing an undervest and a pair of boxing trunks—the ones I bought in Lagos when you said I should take more exercise.

Michel picked up the gold pencil you gave me. It was lying on the table. After a moment he said, "A very nice lady gave you this."

"How do you know that?" I asked.

Another shrug. "I just know it. She is your wife." He paused and added, "She is not in your house now. She is somewhere she does not like to be. Sometimes I know a lot about people which no one has to tell me. Sometimes they are good things. Sometimes they are bad."

"How do you get this information?"

He shook his head. "I don't know," he replied. "I see pictures. But they do not follow each other, one after the other, the way they should.

"Sometimes it is as if I have slipped forward into a life I have not experienced yet and I am hearing a few bars of music out of the middle of a song, but it is not a song I have ever heard before."

Prudence, at McGill University I saw the efforts people are making to reduce everything to calculations they can work out on their slide rules.

That, in fact, is the sort of thing I have been looking for here in my present task.

It is the reason I have sent poor Mamadou off to hunt for a little piece of ribbon because if he finds it, or finds out what has happened to it, especially if it is missing, I shall have a concrete clue to follow up. A piece of ribbon to look for.

My experience with Michel, as I am going to explain, suggests that the greatest mysteries are not related to things we can experience with our five senses.

Certain "gifted" people appear to know things without seeing them or hearing about them.

Michel is evidently one of the "gifted" ones.

He is "tuned in," though his readings, for my purposes, are not yet very good. He is groping. His supernatural insights, he says, come through to him as if he were sitting at a piano striking odd progressions of notes and chords in search of a tune or form upon which to base a composition.

In fact, the little understanding that I have of this gift of his came out during a discussion of his music.

I did not want to press him about his special capabilities, so I told him that I have never come across anyone who seemed, when he sang, to be as totally taken over by his music as he was.

He told me then that his concentration, when he was up in front of the band, made the rhythm and the music as vital to his being as his blood.

He told me that on one occasion, when he was singing, a gas cylinder blew up and that he did not even hear it.

Something like that also happens, he explained, when he tunes in on the supernatural.

You have often asked me, Prudence, what I do when I lie in a sort of trance on my bed looking for the solution of a problem that won't come to me when I use my normal processes and logic. I am letting my kind of music take over.

It is an opening out and a closing in—both at the same time. It is a matter of opening one's mind and throwing out all the garbage that fills it most of the time. For the greatest part of our lives we drown in a flood of trivialities. Then the closing in part is an extraordinary effort of concentration in which we try to blank out all that worthless flood of interference.

Michel has the power to concentrate all his sensibilities to a point where he is clean of all the noise and interference which encrust most people's ability to receive signals that are so delicate that most of us don't even know they exist. And the key to being able to pick them up is concentration, the kind the best of our drummers have. When they are really "there," they burn with concentration and set everyone around them on fire.

You have to hear and watch Michel in front of his band. The power he has over them is more than hypnotic and he drags the other instrumentalists up there with him, making them transcend themselves.

Because he sometimes looks as if he is drugged, I asked him whether he had tried narcotics and whether they had had any effect on him if he had. "The power of drugs is too great to be useful to me. I have to know what I am doing if I am to get the best out of the music. I don't want any force I can't control messing me about."

Then he said, "Forgive me, sir, but we were meant to come together. There is another, too, who should be with us. His spirit is of the cattle people and of Islam."

Amazed, I told him that there is such a one already. I named him and told Michel that the man had been appointed to be my assistant.

"To do what, sir?"

Without waiting for an answer to his question, he told me, "This Mamadou was very disturbed this afternoon."

Which, of course, is true.

After a pause he continued again, "I am not involved with you of my own choice, sir. What I know somewhere here in my head tells me that what I must do, I must do. Even though I feel afraid."

"What are you afraid of?"

"I don't know."

"What has been revealed to you besides what you have told me?"

"That you will be more important in my life than any man I have ever met before. I am caught by the same force that you are, the same gri gri."

I don't know what to make of the young man. "Gri gri" . . . the local word for the occult.

What next? He cannot, or will not, tell me.

I wonder if he is to be trusted. If he is, then his "gift" may be useful.

Like the woman looking at her dead daughter this afternoon, I can only ask, "Why? Why has he been sent to me? By what design? To what end? Death is a drum beating forever . . . Have we been called upon to stop it beating? Or will it beat for us, too?"

There are big, old-fashioned baths attached to these rooms and a huge cylinder of water heated by gas.

Before I sat down to write these last pages for you I soaked for a long time in warm water, and as I lay there a little black cicada joined me. In the water he was as out of his element, as I am in the situation in which I have landed myself here. But he floated well and he kicked with his legs, as he was born to do, and the action propelled him almost as well as a frog propels himself with a similar kick. However, there was no escape for him because, no matter how vigorously he tried, his efforts only brought him up against the polished sides of the bath, which gave him nothing to hold on to so that he could climb out.

I let him swim and closed my eyes.

Then I felt him out of the water on my knee, and before I could move he had jumped clear over the side of the bath and onto the floor.

We seem to be as out of our depth as he was. Shall we also be lucky and escape back to our natural element, as he did?

FOUR

The word has power and the word was "kill."

The pile of jagged boulders stood behind them like a huge splintered tree stump. In the daylight it showed as sunbaked spires and pinnacles standing to a height of nine hundred feet, terracotta in colour, with the plain spread all around their base, flat and yellow.

The women had gone to their sleeping cave not needing to unwind, as the three M's did, from the frenzy which had boiled over them during the orgiastic revelry which had just come to an end.

There had been violence. There always had to be violence, though this evening the object had only been a monkey that had been the subject of the ritual bloodletting. It had been tethered on a rope to a rock and then killed slowly by the women with pointed sticks.

The ceremony had ended with the Master and Broad Tail repeating in public the coupling they had practiced the previous evening.

Kali said drowsily, "You took them all on and you got through to them tonight, brother. I even got the message myself." She was a heavy-breasted woman from Memphis who had started her adult life as the lead singer in a Baptist choir. She had been told then that she had the ability to stand as high, one day, as Mahalia Jackson. That was before she was converted by a certain basilisk-eyed pastor who preached a religion of hate and revenge. He had worked hard on her and suddenly it had been like a spiritual conversion to God, only instead of exalting her, it brought her, as she put it, down to being on first-name terms with the devil.

In Arrani the same hate had been distilled by his intellect out of cold reason and fanatical study. He was the only one of the three who was at home in Transniger. He had been born there. Scholarships had taken him to France and then to America, where he had written a Ph.D. thesis on "Total Alienation, the Divorce of the

Afro-American from his Cultural Heritage." It had not been accepted, though parts of it had been printed in *La Voix d'Afrique Occidental.* It had been a white professor, a "liberal," who had turned it down. Arrani knew that academically he had made a good case. Most Afro-Americans could not go back to Africa even if they wanted to, because what they wanted more than anything else was to be accepted as Americans. If they could bleach their skins, take the curls out of their hair and change their features, they would. However it had had to be a white who had told him, in effect, that he did not know what he was talking about . . . a man who had not been to West Africa and seen the Afros' malaise when they came back to the countries where their families had originated, or the way the "white niggers" lorded it over the blacks in Liberia. Most of them came, did not like what they saw, and went back home again—"home" being the U.S.A. A few did stay and merge happily with their black kin, but they were the exception rather than the rule.

The root of his own trouble had been that it had always been a white, like the professor who had turned down his thesis, who had offered superior judgements on the work he had done, had told him "no" or "you can't" or "smart-ass blacks ain't needed around here, boy." It was also unfortunately true that he felt isolated from most of his own people, feeling that he knew more than any others about the road the blacks had been forced to travel by the whites for more than four hundred years. Or, if they knew the story, they could treat it with indifference whereas he could not.

And so, alone with his "unacceptable" thesis in his hand, he had come to the end of the road and had, by chance, met the man he now called Hassan ben Salah, the Big M. The effect had been as if someone had put a sharp knife in his hand just when he felt like cutting everyone's throat. The man boiled over with a force of character which Arrani himself lacked, and he was very, very discontented.

At that time the Big M's name had been Booker West, and Lindy Spence—now Kali—had already found in his brutal strength and vigour a man who complemented her own hunger for power and the satisfaction she could take from it and use herself.

He, Arrani, had been responsible for all of them changing their names. He had made a start on this process when he had told them that Booker T. Washington, for whom the Big M had been named, was the first Uncle Tom. He had suggested that Booker could make himself respectable, if he wanted to be named for a black hero, if he took Marcus Garvey as his patron. So after that, for a while, it had been Marcus Garvey, Lindy Spence and Askia Dan Sori, the name which appeared on his passport. Then, over a series of nights he had told them the story of the white man's exploitation of the blacks, not just the bits and pieces which they knew, but the history in detail, starting with the arrival of the first Portuguese on the West African coast and carrying on right up to the present economic pressures from outside which ensure continued foreign domination and underdevelopment.

Booker West, alias Marcus Garvey, alias Hassan ben Salah, the Big M, had kept saying, "Is that so, man?" and, "You have to be kidding," as Arrani had given them detailed accounts of the slave trade and the treatment of slaves in the West Indies, Brazil and the U.S.A. Christian missionaries in Barbados, he had told them, had had their slaves, men and women, branded so that everyone would know who they belonged to. And the captain of a British slave ship, the *Zong*, had had an outbreak of dysentery on board, so he had thrown his whole cargo of men, women and children overboard in mid-Atlantic and had then tried to claim insurance on them as spoiled cargo.

"You have to be kidding."

There had been much more: about the bloody brutality of King Leopold of the Belgians; about the way the Portuguese replaced slavery with indentured labour, which even further lowered the value of a black man's life because he could be replaced from stock; about the Sharpsville massacre in South Africa and the cruelties of the Boer farmers who drove their labourers in the fields with rhinoceros-hide whips; about the "black fruit" which hung from the trees after a Louisiana lynching party, and he showed them a photograph of a lot of white, grinning men, women and children standing in front of an orchard bearing that kind of fruit. There had, of course, been much more until finally the Big M had said, "They ought to be killed. The whole goddam lot of the white sons of bitches ought to be killed."

To which he, Arrani, had replied, "When do we start?"

And Kali had asked, "And where?"

"We have to be practical," had been the Big M's response, "make a master plan and stay with it." And they had all three suddenly realised that they had spoken in deadly seriousness.

From then on, they had applied themselves . . . planning.

The Big M had at once recommenced his reading under Arrani's tutelage, and together, often reading aloud to each other, they had read every book they could find about killing from works on the Assassins and Thugs, through Canetti's Auto-da-Fé, down to the earliest books on Manson.

Along the way, the Big M had found that he could play with words; only, as Arrani had pointed out, in Africa words were not things you played with, words were power in the truest form of that statement. In Africa, he had explained, the word is regarded as something which makes things, whether they are good or bad, come alive. They are the roots from which everything that has life grows.

"Is that so, brother?"

Kali had shaken her head and had said, "What you have in that gourd of yours, brother, beats everything."

"Incantations, exorcisms, blessings, curses—they are all word magic." Arrani had continued, "If you want to control people politically, through the occult or in any other way, you have to use words. You have to tell yourself, 'I want that man dead,' if you want to act from the basis of a plan. Action can be a reflex; then you don't know what's happening or what you are doing. Or you can use action consciously to gain power, then you have to use words."

So here they were celebrating another assassination. The plan was working. The word has power and the word was "kill."

And dealing again with words he had suggested, after they had arrived in Africa, that they all change their names to give them related power, and he had chosen the ones each of them should adopt.

Hassan ben Salah, the Big M's name, had belonged to a man who had lived about the time that William the Conqueror had invaded England. He was said to have combined the religious fervour of St. Augustine with the political astuteness of Lenin. He founded the Order of the Assassins, a sect which held that murder was a religious duty, following predecessors who had held the same creed and had strangled their victims with cords.

Kali was the dark mother Goddess of Time and the Saviour of the Universe. She represented terror and motherly tenderness, death and creation, and she was revered by the Thugs, another sect which murdered by strangulation, each of those whom they killed being dedicated as a religious sacrifice to Kali.

Arrani, rather contemptuously, named himself Bu Tahir Arrani, in commemoration of one of the Assassins who won fame and death by murdering the greatest threat to their cult, the Grand Vizier of Malik Shah, Nizam Al-Mulk.

From lounging against a rock the Big M suddenly sat up and said,

"Hey, I forgot to tell you. They are turning that guy Quarshie loose to find out who is doing the killing."

While they had been living in Port St. Mary, before they came north, Quarshie had tracked down a murderer and had scotched a plot which could have led to civil war in Akhana. They had also heard stories around the marketplace of a couple of other murders in which he had brought the killers to one sort of justice or another.

Arrani took off his glasses and wiped them. Then as he put them on again, he said, "You and Kali ought to be able to put him off the trail. If you can't, we might set up a contest amongst the girls to see who will be the first to put his neck in a noose. You don't scare me with that kind of information, brother."

"I wasn't trying to scare you. I just wanted to see if you would react to it the same way I did."

"And did I?"

"Yes, sir, you did. You know, he travelled up on the bus with that old Englishman. Pity we didn't get onto that information earlier. It might have saved us the trouble of setting up something now." The Big M got up, yawned and stretched. "Well, I'm for the sack," he concluded, "I've had a kind of busy evening."

FIVE

. . . a carrier of bad news . . .

I am sure Dababa, if he had studied my activities today, would not only wonder if the word "method" meant anything at all to me but would also think that I am delinquent, Quarshie wrote his wife. *Yet I am sure that what I did was sensible, even if there is nothing tangible to show for it.*

Today was spent devoting all my efforts to trying to understand my two assistants. I started the day with Mamadou and spent the whole morning with him. Then in the late afternoon and early evening I spent several hours with Michel.

I think it is right to say that they both had some special urge to work with me. Mamadou was motivated by status and wanted to establish me in the "father of the house" relationship I told you about earlier. Michel was prompted by a feeling he cannot describe with any exactitude, but I know it had to do with his mediumistic, occult, superpsychic—or whatever the right word is—powers.

So . . . Mamadou, first.

I asked him to take me on a tour of his town and then to his house to show me some of his poetry.

We set out at eight o'clock and already the heat was beginning to lean heavily on my shoulders. It had been a restless night with the diesel locomotive shunting furiously, a cowboy film at the movies, and Michel, with his five-piece rhythm section, making the foundations of this old building shake.

Mamadou was nervous. He is very highly strung, despite his languid manner.

His hands probably say more about him than his face does. They are very fine boned, very long and inert, passive and, on the rare occasions when he does use them to gesticulate, they are the careful hands of a classical scholar. Does that make sense? They are the hands of a perfectionist.

He is also, in his own right, a very important person and was greeted everywhere we went like a princeling.

We visited the marketplace first. You would not feel at home there at all, Prudence. It is not like our markets, it is much more formal. There are few women because, of course, this is a Muslim area and the women, except for the most humble, do not go out very much. Probably ninety per cent of the people one would see in our markets would be women; here it is just the reverse.

Our markets divide roughly into three sections of equal size: one third for food, one third for cloth, and one third for everything else, including fetish and herbal medicines, hardware, toiletry goods and so on.

Here it is local handicrafts—weaving, leatherwork, beaten copper and brassware, wood carving and pottery which predominate. The roofed area is circular, with a gangway between the booths which are set up around the hub of the circle. In the middle there is a tiled fountain. And it is quiet, even dignified. The few women who have stalls are located outside in the roadway and the hot sun.

Everywhere bearded elders and younger men dressed in white or blue robes, like Mamadou's, put their hands together and bowed to him as he passed by. Most scrupulously he returned the bows.

We passed a mosque which opened, like the shops on each side of it, onto the main road. Mamadou asked me to wait a moment and went inside.

It is a very simple building with beautiful tiles on the walls and a smooth, clean, tiled floor. There is nothing else in it except a few old men seated around the wide arch where I waited, and a few others saying their prayers.

Mamadou joined them facing towards Mecca. He stood, bowed from the waist, knelt, leant forward and put his forehead on the floor and repeated these movements three or four times. Then he walked quickly to the entrance, kicked his feet into his shoes, which he had left there, and rejoined me with, I think, a lighter step.

He took me down to the banks of the Niger. It was by now roasting hot.

All along the banks, where they could be watered easily, there were small patches of cultivated land, mostly bearing vegetables. Beyond these little gardens the riverbanks were lined with people washing themselves and their clothes, which they spread out beside them to dry, so that there was a wide mosaic of colours right in front of us and stretching to the right and left as far as the eye could see. On the other bank there was the same scene with the water, between these two ribbons of colour, a deep shade of blue which came close to that of the blue ink we used to buy when I was a schoolboy.

Mamadou talked nervously all the time, not about the town but about the way he was taught as a child.

"Be accurate in repeating the words of your Lord," his instructor kept telling him, "for they were pronounced by the Master of the World. You, miserable child, must repeat them perfectly, following Him. And you shall suffer until you speak them as He demanded that they be spoken. The master used to twist my ears until the tears ran down my cheeks from the pain, but he never allowed me to make a mistake, not even one. You see, he believed that God is so exalted that it is pure wickedness not to pronounce the words of the Koran perfectly, even for a child who does not understand them—and certainly at that time I understood only a very small proportion of them. And he drove me harder than he drove all the others, because of my parentage and the fact that I did learn better than the others. Also, I was to be his salvation. He was an old man, and when he faced God after his death he was determined that he would be able to say truthfully that he had had one perfect pupil."

Then Mamadou talked of the trouble he is having because his family want him to take a wife.

"I have read a great deal," he told me. "I read and write English as well as French and Arabic, and I know that others would think that our marriage customs are strange. I, too, am beginning to wonder about them. My wife will have to live like a prisoner, and if I do not find her satisfactory I may get rid of her simply by saying, 'I divorce you,' three times. I may then go and find a new wife. She must wait a hundred days before she seeks a new husband.

"There are many women who have been divorced eight or nine times, and such ones are easy to come by as wives. There are only a few who have not been divorced at least two or three times. And when I marry it will be my duty to decide everything which relates to our life together. Until a girl marries she must obey her parents, and after that her husband. We shall avoid using each other's names in conversation. She will walk behind me wherever we go and speak to me as little as possible in the presence of other people. If somebody visits us I must meet them at the door and my wife must disappear." Then Mamadou put his chin up and faced straight ahead. "But

the question of marriage is not one on which I can take advice," he concluded. "It is one in which I must make my own decision."

We went to his house. Like many of the homes of the well-to-do here, it is built in the Moorish style with all the rooms facing inwards towards a central courtyard. Inside it is almost cool.

He said, when we had seated ourselves on some low cushions in the cloister in front of his room, "It is quite widely known, sir, that you drink beer. In my house I can offer it to you, but I may not make that offer outside."

"What will you drink?" I ask.

"Coca-Cola."

Who was it who said, "The basic objective of the West in Africa is to convert a taste for water into a taste for Coca-Cola"?

I took beer.

Then shyly he said, "You asked about my poetry. Most of it is written in Arabic. It is a difficult language for those who do not know it, and difficult to translate because there is much that people might call wordplay in it. You know about this, perhaps?"

I shook my head.

"Then let me explain. I will take four letters, consonants . . . K H D and R. Adding vowels and sometimes the consonant L and changing the order of the root letters K H D and R, which in themselves already have an unspoken meaning, I can make eight words. Each of them will have a meaning which is in some way related to the original root meaning. Then behind each first-level meaning there are other symbolic meanings, sometimes three or four." And he went on eagerly to demonstrate. I followed him, but with difficulty. No wonder the Arabs invented algebra. You have to know and understand all the rules or you will never make any of their literary equations come out. No wonder, too, Mamadou's teacher bullied him into developing a perfect memory.

After I told him I thought I had understood the gist of what he had been telling me, he went away and came back with a book bound in green leather with an elaborately tooled design on it in gold.

Pointing to the design with his long, slender finger he told me, "I followed the work of a master when I developed this. They say that such a pattern, which at the same time repeats itself and transforms itself, is symbolic of eternity."

Then he opened the book and said, "These are some of my poems. As you see, they are written in Kufic script."

I looked at his hands and then at the text, and I knew that for all their fine bones they had a strength of control and precision which must be very rare. The writing is put down as decisively and gracefully as nature herself draws lines in an orchid or in shadows on water.

"I like the Sufi poets best," he told me. "They are the great masters. This poem, here, I can translate quite easily because the thought is a simple one." He pointed to a page. "I wrote it following some reading I had been doing of Maulana Jalaluddin Rumi."

I made him write the translation down for me. Here it is.

"Rumi proclaims that all in the Koran
Is Allegory,
That it has seven meanings.
Maulana Jalaluddin Rumi,
I am your very humble servant.
Seven is overrich for my poor mind.
Teach me to understand just one meaning
That I may not fail the final test
As a man, who is given a bow with seven strings,
May be killed before he can decide to which one
He should string his arrow."

I have a warm feeling for the boy, now—boy, he is perhaps twenty-five. From the beginning I have been wronging him. I told him, "Mamadou, you will one day be a very great man. You have all the gifts that are necessary to make one."

To which he replied, "I know. That is, all except the one which you can give me . . . self-confidence." He was not being boastful. As he saw it, he was simply stating a fact.

Michel's story is quite different. Mamadou was born into a condition in which he had nothing to do except to form his own character.

They are both gifted, but Mamadou never had to use his gifts for such practical purposes as filling his belly. He was also born to receive respect.

Michel has had to fight not only for his life but for simple recognition as a human being. And he has had to do both carrying a handicap that is about as bitter as it could be. He is a living travesty, a ghost. His deformity causes him much the same problems that he would have if he had an obvious case of leprosy. People avoid him.

Children run away from him. He is not considered to be of this world but rather a changeling, a familiar attending a witch or some sort of spirit.

It is not surprising that he was alarmed when he found that he was outside the normal run of human beings in other ways as well, that is, that he is clairvoyant. He began to wonder if the view other people had of him was not true, after all, and that he was truly a creature that had been born into the wrong element.

He took me to the compound where he has a room.

He does not qualify for any of the strangers' zongos.

The compound belongs to a good woman. She is not a Muslim but is very dark-skinned and fat.

"Everywhere I went," he told me, "they wanted to charge double or treble the normal rent. They were afraid that because I was there other people would stay away—that is, when they were not actually frightened of me."

It is like the stories your brother told, Prudence, of trying to find a room near his work in England. He had a black face amongst whites, Michel has a white face amongst blacks—and both were expected to pay triple.

The compound owner greeted me respectfully and sent one of her children to fetch some beer for us with money I gave her.

Michel occupies one small room. It is whitewashed, has a bed and a chair and a wooden box to hold his clothes and other possessions. He also has a cassette tape recorder standing on the floor beside a kerosene lamp. The room is very neat, clean and tidy.

I sat on the box. He sat on the bed and we used the chair for the bottles of beer.

"She is strange," Michel said, after the woman had left the room. "She mothers me. It has never happened to me before. Or, perhaps, she nurses me. She is even rather proud of me and brings her friends to hear me sing. In the band it is all right, too. André—he plays the trumpet—he and I work well together. Each can feel what the other wants to do. You said it is only a pretty good band, sir. It is a very good band."

I told him, "Of course it is a very good band. But it is only good because you make it good. If you left it would only be a competent rhythm section and a trumpeter." Then I asked him where he was born, how he came to find out that he had a gift for music.

His parents were slaves brought up here from a village much further south. Their master was a black Muslim, and his father was for-

tunate not to have been shipped East to the Nile Valley or to the Arabian coast. Michel's father served this Muslim so well that he became steward of all his master's property and was then given his liberty and a privileged position in the village. When that happened he took a wife who bore him Michel.

The woman was delivered of her son in a convent hospital which was served by French nuns, and she left him there because neither she nor her husband wanted an albino child. She later had other sons and daughters and thus flushed the shame of having given birth to him out of her system.

The nuns had been kind and practical. His eyes, of course, were weak and he could not stand the sun, which made his skin painfully red. So they taught him French and English and also how to cook à la Française. *He had worked in the convent kitchen until he was fifteen, and then he went to work at a house which was occupied by a community of White Fathers.*

One day one of the Fathers heard him singing hymns while he was working. There was an old foot-operated harmonium in the house, and this Father—he was a French-Canadian—had taught him how to read and play music. After three years, as well as being the cook, he was also the community organist.

As an aside he told me that when they had earned enough money, the band was going to buy an electric organ which he would play as he sang.

Then an American Peace Corps worker, doing a soil survey, came to stay at the community. The young man had had a tape recorder and a lot of cassettes of secular music. "And I woke up," Michel told me. "Just as the Fathers knew that serving their mission was their calling, I discovered that the kind of music we make here is for me. I earn better money than most. I enjoy my work because I understand it and it comes very easily to me. Also, I can work at night so that I am not bothered by the sun. Fate was unkind to make me white, but she gave me back something for what she took away. She gave me music. Now if I was told that I could have my proper skin colour but that I would have to give up my music for it, I would say, 'Keep your skin colour.' "

"And when were you first aware that you had the power to be clairvoyant?"

"Not long ago. A little while after I moved into this compound. I had had malaria and I was depressed. I was lying here in my bed feel-

ing weak and miserable, and I found myself in what I thought was a dream, but I knew I was awake.

"I could see the light shining through the jalousies all the time. It attacked as if a hand were clawing at my back and scalp, and I felt afraid. Then the room seemed to fill up with noise and dust, and there was the edge of a cliff and something forced me to look over it. The dust turned red and there was mud in the road with pools of blood in it. At the bottom of the cliff there was a fire. That was what was making the dust red. Beside me there was a low wall which was broken. Then behind me I heard cries and moans. There was a fire there, too, that made a flickering light in the dust. I tried to move towards the cries but my feet were fixed on the ground. Presently the dust cleared a little and I saw the wheels of a mammy wagon and they were pointing up into the air. The worst thing was that I knew there was nothing that I could do. I could not move and I knew that there was something worse that was going to happen."

"The child, who went to fetch our beer, came in then bringing me food, and she said afterwards that she thought the malaria had come back and I was delirious because I was groaning and sweating and saying, 'Stop. Stop.' "

"And?" I prompted him when he did not speak for several moments.

He sighed, shook his head and continued, "A little way up the river from Fort Etienne the ground rises to a plateau and the road to Ougadougou climbs the scarp in a series of hairpin bends. It is very narrow and on one side the cliff goes straight up, and on the other it falls away down a steep slope.

"At the time when I was lying here 'dreaming,' a sand storm was blowing up there and two lorries, loaded with people, collided on a bend. One went down over the edge, and the other turned upside down. Another lorry coming down the hill ran into the wreck on the road. Forty people were killed. Many, many others were injured, and I was there and I knew the other lorry was coming. That was why I was shouting, 'Stop.' "

There was sweat on Michel's forehead. He swallowed a lot of beer, closed his eyes and concluded, "I learned next day that a man I knew very well had been killed in the accident."

I let him sit quietly for quite a long time and he drank some more beer.

Eventually I asked him, "After that terrible experience has anything like it ever happened again?"

He shook his head. "Small things," he said. "Comfort, the woman who owns the compound—it is not her real name, but it is what I call her—Comfort lost a gold bracelet and I told her where it was. André, the trumpeter, was worried one day because his wife had not come back from her village where she had gone to visit her parents, and I knew that there had been a death there and that she had had to stay for the funeral. Twice I have seen things which happened after I spoke of them. I saw a friend off at the station one day and he said, 'In two days I will be in Miwiville.' I told him that it would not be so, that there would be trouble between Fort Etienne and the coast and he would be several days late. The train was derailed at Ebongé. No one was hurt, but they were held up for a long while. The other time the guitarist you met was going to go back to visit his family, and I told him not to go because there was danger. Because of what I had told the friend who took the train to Miwiville, he listened and stayed in Fort Etienne. Later we heard that there was cholera in his village. It is strange, I don't have to think about these things, except for a tiny moment when I am aware of nothing else. It lasts no longer than a flash of lightning. For that moment I am dead, and then the idea, a picture, is there. I saw the friend who was in the derailment squatting beside the tracks fanning a cooking fire. And I saw police stopping traffic on the road to the guitarist's village."

Prudence, the capabilities which Michel seems to have are something new to me. Of course, I have heard of people with similar powers. I have seen the way our diviners work with their "accept the verdict of the bones" approach, or the verdict of the cowrie shells or kola nuts or whatever other instruments they use, like those Irish friends I had in Canada who used playing cards or tea leaves. But Michel's capabilities are different. The method of prediction is different. Our diviners are usually asked questions to which the answer is largely "yes" or "no." Is the time propitious for doing this or that? Is she a witch? Am I bewitched? I don't have a child; is this because I have done something wrong? Am I in trouble because I have broken a taboo?

Michel is not involved with any mediumistic palaver. He is not talking with an ancestor or some other control.

He is seeing the future, not telling it. He moves forward in time and sees an event that is going to happen the day after tomorrow as if the Muslim belief in predestination is true and he can tap into it.

What am I to believe? That he is involved in some sort of trick-

ery? That he is the master of coincidence and can make it work for him?

I have more questions than answers.

One answer is, of course, that we humans have more latent powers than we have yet discovered. Also that those with a certain kind of insight or genius have an exceptional control over disconnected ideas and can bring unlikely elements together to produce results which are not only unlikely but improbable.

So my conclusion is not to try to worry out answers but just to accept Michel's gift as one more mystery in a world full of mysteries. And to be grateful for them.

I asked him when it was he got his feelings about me—that is, about the way our relationship was going to develop.

"When I saw your picture in the paper," he replied. "I knew that we would meet and"—he looked down at the liver-coloured blotches on his white hands—"and that you would have a big influence on my life. I also knew that we would share danger together."

"Danger from what?"

"I don't know. I have told you my knowledge is often incomplete. Somehow I feel that you will be in more danger than I will and that, in a way which I cannot explain, it stands behind you."

"Is that all?"

"Yes, sir. And this is where I feel that I am no good. I only have half the capability I should have and I am afraid that it is something like my white skin—it could be hurtful to me. It seems as if I am a carrier of bad news, like men who carry disease."

"If you ask me," I told him to comfort him, "you are particularly sensitive to the forces of evil; therefore you will be a very welcome friend to many people because you can warn them when there is danger. Come, we will go and have some dinner at the hotel." And when he stood up I put my arm around his shoulders and I knew then why Comfort mothered him. He was more than the orphan his abandonment by his parents had made him; he was an outcast who was hungry for the kind of physical contact no one else ever gave him. He held himself stiff for a moment and then relaxed against me and stood like that for several seconds before he moved away.

As he locked the door of his room he said, speaking rather carefully, "I was given a white skin and to compensate for it, music. I am given the power to step dangerously close, as you said, to evil, and a *new friend who behaves as a father to me. So there must be some sort of intelligence in the world which balances good against evil."*

When we got back to the hotel the barman gave me a note which said, "See me immediately, please. Dababa."

I drank a beer with Michel, ate a very quick meal with him, took a taxi, picked up Mamadou and went to the newspaper office.

Dababa was not there, but a clerk was on the lookout for me. He gave me an envelope. Inside it there was a message which read: "To shoot down your enemies in the street may be unprecedented, but I was looking for results, not precedents. How did Napoleon win his victories? He took his opponents in the flank or rear. And what is right on the grand scale is not wrong when the scale is reduced and the odds against you are a hundred to one." Those are the words of General George Grivas. The odds against us are millions to one, but we shall overcome as the following equations prove. The sword = the garrotte. The dynamic which X exploits = the dynamic which we use. He works for profit. We work for retribution. He has been judged guilty of murder by proxy. We, by moral right, are his executioners. His conscience is foul with sin. Ours will be as clear as the sky at dawn tomorrow."

I read the message several times and knew that I would have to think about it very carefully. They, whoever they were, were obviously overconfident. "Hypertrophy of the ego. These patients project . . . an ego that is clumsy and domineering . . . Their pride is characteristic . . ." Adler? Or someone else I read as part of my studies.

"I have to think," I told Mamadou. "The hotel is too noisy. Where can I go where I can think in peace and quiet?"

"My room, sir. In my house," he replied. "It is where I meditate."

As a footnote to the above, Prudence, I think it must be evident that my feelings for both these young men have quickly developed into real affection. We Africans are more lucky than we know. We can develop "loving" bonds without the relationships being stigmatised as sexual. Physical contact is important in the relationship, but at root these are feelings of kinship. This is because amongst our people the sexes have always been so widely segregated that our need for love has had to spill over into our relationships with others of our own sex.

Of course, with Mamadou and Michel, the explanation of my feelings for them—and perhaps theirs for me—does not involve what I have just said above. In their case they are seeking a father of the house, and my heart tells me to recognise them as sons. So, Prudence, in this at least we are lucky. From being childless we have, in a matter of months, acquired three sons—first Arimi, and now Mamadou and Michel.

SIX

I wonder how it feels to be looking into a man's eyes, from only an inch or two away, as he dies.

Quarshie found that Mamadou's room had the austerity of a monk's cell. It contained a bed, a chair, a cupboard, a bedside table with a lamp on it, and one decoration on the wall at the end of the bed. It was a reproduction of part of a text, written in Kufic script with the statement printed chromatically in the colour of dried blood. The lines of text were divided by an intricate arabesque pattern done, on a pale-blue background, in gold leaf. The walls were white and the furniture was made of unpainted wood so that the eye was always taken back to the room's one decoration.

"What is it?" asked Quarshie. "A quotation from the Koran?"

"*Danad o ki nekbakht wa muharam ast:*

"*Ziraki az Iblis ishq Adam ast.*" Mamadou read the words aloud.

"It is the work of the Sufi poet Rumi again. Roughly it translates as, 'He who is fortunate enough to have seen the light . . .' That is, a man who is a Sufi. '. . . knows that fraudulence comes from the devil, and love from Adam.' You may find that my bed is rather hard, sir, and I can get you a pillow if you want one."

Quarshie took the young man's slender hand in his great fist and told him, "I have never entered a room that has more to give than this one. And what the room has to give is what you have given to it. Thank you, my friend."

Mamadou bowed slightly and replied, "Thank you, sir. What you have said makes me very happy."

He turned away and left the room, closing the door quietly.

Barshun'a had been established.

Quarshie took off his jacket—it was not the kind which needed a shirt to be worn with it—kicked off his shoes and socks and lay on the bed. The windows were open and the jalousies were closed.

Outside there was a lamp in the courtyard, and light from it filtered through the slats in the jalousies, one bar of it falling dramatically on the Sufi quotation which hung on the wall.

Quarshie closed his eyes. Something in the message Dababa had received had sown a seed which stimulated a tiny spark in his memory.

He reviewed the quotation. A sword equals a garrotte. Those who live by the sword do not die by the sword but by the garrotte. Could that be what the first equation meant? Those who live by the sword would be soldiers. Were they talking about the General, or was there a white military man in Fort Etienne? An attaché at one of the embassies, maybe? If the message referred to the General, they had to be bluffing . . . "they." Yes. The message kept talking about "we." So that was the first piece of solid evidence that the murders were being committed by more than one man. Just in case they did have some idea of an attempt on the General's life, his guards had better take extra security precautions.

He got up, opened one of the jalousies and looked out into the courtyard. Mamadou was sitting on one of the big mattresslike cushions in the cloister. He came across to Quarshie the moment he saw him.

"Contact your uncle, the Chef de Cabinet," Quarshie told him. "Say that we have received this message and that it would be sensible to alert the General's guards to the possibility of an attempt on his life. Underline that it is only a possibility and that I doubt very much that the threat is directed against the President. Though, of course, we must take precautions against every possibility. Tell him I am still working on an interpretation of the message and will let him know as soon as I have anything I can be sure of."

When he was alone again, Quarshie returned to bed and to his speculation.

"The dynamic X exploits = the dynamic we use."

Assuming that when they speak of "dynamic" they mean force, Quarshie pondered, then the force X uses, whoever he is—perhaps the intended victim—is the same as the force the assassins use. The garrotte? No, but the use of the garrotte involves violence. Work with that. X uses violence, which would still fit with his being a soldier. But he works for profit. To make a profit you usually have to sell something. Soldiers do not normally sell things, so X is someone who sells force. Not garrottes but the sword, which are both weapons of violence. Arms. An arms salesman. The General had spoken of an

American arms salesman who was being watched by the Russian who had been strangled. Surely an arms salesman who was a natural quarry for anyone seeking retribution against an enemy could be said to kill by proxy and should have a conscience foul with sin.

He relaxed, clearing his mind, but found that there was still a fragment of the problem left. "As clear as dawn tomorrow." He opened his eyes and saw the quotation in Kufic script at the end of the bed. Staring at it he remembered Mamadou's translation,

"He who is fortunate enough to have seen the light."

Fortunate enough to have seen the light . . . our conscience will be as clear as the sky at dawn *tomorrow*. Why tomorrow?

And then, in a moment, he was struggling into his jacket shouting, "Mamadou. Mamadou."

He was pulling on his socks as the young man's long face with an expression of alarm on it peered around the door.

"Mamadou, we have no time to waste. The General mentioned that there was a white man here who is a small-arms salesman. He is the man they are after and the job will be done tonight. Get your uncle on the phone again. I must speak to him."

A few moments later a cool voice said, "Yes, Doctor?"

Quarshie took a deep breath and measured the tone of his voice against the tone adopted by the unexcitable Chef de Cabinet.

"I think we are going to have to move rather fast, monsieur," he said. "I have that warning note worked out. The killers—there is more than one of them—will try to kill the American arms salesman the General spoke to me about." He paused and added slowly and deliberately, "The attempt will take place before dawn tomorrow."

"Ah. You are sure?"

"Who can be sure when we are obviously dealing with people who are pathological? Anyway, maintain the careful surveillance of His Excellency and give me that man's address if you have it, please."

The dry voice said, "I can do better than that, Doctor. We have him under watch day and night, a two-man guard all the time. So if he is not at home we shall know exactly where he is. By the time you and Mamadou reach the Residence I shall have the information you need."

Ten minutes later the Chef de Cabinet said, "He took a Trans-nigerian girl to the Hotel Independence for dinner. They are not in the dining room any more, nor have they left the hotel."

"Did he book a room?"

"No."

"Tell me something about the man."

"Middle-aged, American. What his fellow countrymen call a wheeler-dealer, isn't it?" The Chef de Cabinet accented heavily the last syllables of the two words wheeler-dealer. "We don't like him, but we cannot get any firm evidence that he is involved in anything illegal such as the supply of guns to criminals, or anything like that. However, there are people just over the frontier—not our people, you understand—who have received quite a large consignment of automatic arms and ammunition. I have passed this information on to my colleagues over there. Officially the man works for the A.M.S. Tractor and Heavy Equipment Supply Company from Birmingham, Alabama. All his papers are in order and the only activity he undertakes here that we view with disfavour is his habit of using and then discarding our women."

"A little habit which could be the death of him." Quarshie was not smiling as he repeated the cliché. "Your man is sure he has not come out."

"Since these murders started we have put a high wire fence all around the building. There is only one way out or in, and there are police on duty there."

"Then he must still be in there. We will go and look for him. Would you get on to the police and ask them to send four men to the hotel, please?"

"No more?"

"Four men should be able to handle two women."

"He only went in with one."

Quarshie was self-conscious because he knew he was showing off. There was something about the Chef de Cabinet that made him want to shake the man's complacency.

"And I suspect that he will come out feet first without any at all. I will telephone you if we find that my suspicions are confirmed. Then you can relax some of the vigilance here. Would you rather we found the man dead or alive?"

"Either way he will present problems, complications with the U. S. Government. Perhaps they will be less if he is dead."

After checking at the reception desk at the hotel, Quarshie asked to see the manager, who at once recognised him and his companion and invited them into his office. He was a Frenchman, brusque, businesslike and prepared to co-operate with someone so closely associated with the President.

After an exchange of formalities he said, "I feel fortunate, Doctor, because I never have to leave the premises here. My friends tell me that when they are outside they are always looking over their shoulders. It is an unhappy condition to be in, no? Now, what can I do for you, monsieur?"

Quarshie wondered if the man would still feel so secure after they had carried out their search of the building.

He said, "It is a rather delicate matter, monsieur. We may have to search all the rooms in the hotel."

"What for, Doctor?"

"To find if there is an American gentleman, a Mr. Edgar P. Kerrigan, occupying one of your rooms without being registered. I checked the book at the reception desk as we came in."

The manager shrugged. "I would not try to deceive you, Doctor. My staff take bribes and arrange that the things for which they take them do not come to my attention. Experienced men are hard to find and it is just the experienced ones who take the bribes and know how to get away with it. If I may suggest it, I will telephone all the rooms from my office here and warn people that we are coming so that they can be prepared for us and will not be alarmed."

Quarshie shook his head. "No, I am sorry, monsieur. Then we might find that our time, yours and mine, has been wasted. The birds will have been warned and will have flown away. You have a passkey, do you not?"

"Yes, Doctor, I have." The manager spoke without enthusiasm. "May I ask what you expect to find?"

"Mr. Kerrigan."

"Then, why not use the telephone?"

"Because he may not be able to answer it."

"*Nom d'un nom*, why?"

"One of the facts of death, monsieur, is that it causes a man to lose his voice."

"You are serious? There is a dead man in this hotel?"

"The longer we talk about it the more likelihood there is that he will be killed."

"*Quelle horreur*. We must go with all quickness. Come."

The hotel, which was the latest addition to the skyline in Fort Etienne, had over two hundred rooms, many of them, because the hot season was approaching, untenanted.

Even the few rooms which were booked were mostly empty, and the only incident that occurred before they found Mr. Kerrigan was the discovery, in what should have been an empty room, of an older man and a youth.

Since both men were black, the manager's straight-faced comment, that neither of the two men could be Mr. Kerrigan, became more macabre than humorous when they actually found Kerrigan.

The body of the late Edgar P. Kerrigan, dressed only in his undershirt, was lying face down on a bed with the hook and eye of a garrotte exactly over the vertebrae at the back of his neck and with the toggles on the ends of the instrument placed neatly between his shoulder blades.

Quarshie rolled the body partially on its back and glanced at the stains on the sheet underneath the man.

"Caught in the act," he said. "There must have been two girls. The one underneath him probably held his body as close to her as she could, and at that moment her friend slipped a noose over his head and pulled it tight. The one who handled the garrotte might have pressed down on his back with her hands to hold him still until he was dead." Rather harshly he added, "I wonder how it feels to be looking into a man's eyes, from only an inch or two away, as he dies. Monsieur," he told the hotel manager, who had sat down rather suddenly on the bench provided for suitcases, "one of your staff not only took a bribe, he could also, to stretch a point a very little bit, be considered to be an accomplice in a murder. You will please co-operate with the police, as you have so perfectly co-operated with me, to find that man. I will arrange with the police to collect the man's body so that I can do an autopsy. I would like to know for certain whether this garrotte is deadly because it works on the carotid arteries or because it ruptures the thyroid cartilage."

Then Quarshie turned to Mamadou and said, "There is a lot of work for you, my friend. I want you to get a full picture of what happened here tonight, to find how the girls got away, if they did indeed get away, or where they are now, if they did not. They must both have been seen. Find out the time they arrived, how they behaved, whether anyone saw who picked them up when they left the hotel, and any other details you think would be useful to our investigation. You will use the four policemen by sending two to reinforce the men who are on the gate to make certain that no one leaves this building until you have questioned them. The other two will help you. Keep people out of bed, or get them out of bed, if you have to. I will have a man sent over who will check this room for footprints and fingerprints. Until then, lock the door and don't let anyone in. I will also have the Superintendent send over his best sergeant. Will that be enough to keep you busy? I don't have to tell you that I have complete faith in your ability to carry out my orders. You will probably do a more thorough job than I would."

Down in the lobby Quarshie shook hands with the manager and said to him, "Au revoir, monsieur." The man had obviously been shattered by the experience, so Quarshie said, comfortingly, "My assistant will be discreet and try to cause as little trouble for you as possible in the way he deals with your customers. He is a very intelligent and sensitive young man."

In fact, after calling at the police station to see the Superintendent and to (in the French Ambassador's phrase) "fill him in" on the situation, Quarshie returned to the Hotel Buffet de la Gare and called the Chef de Cabinet from the reception desk, where the one telephone in the hotel was located.

Quarshie said, "You got your wish."

"Perhaps I should not have made a wish. I should have enough faith in your intellectual and intuitive powers not to treat them as a joke, as you do. That is a very remarkable skill you have, Doctor."

"It would be even more remarkable if it could get me to a location where I am needed before it is occupied by a corpse."

"Even when it belongs—belonged—to a lecherous arms salesman?"

"Yes, even then. I would prefer to see him and all his kin tried as accomplices in mass murder, convicted and *then* garrotted."

"Yet you told H.E. that you are not a violent man."

"You have his office bugged."

"With his knowledge and for his own protection. He can turn the microphone off, if he wants to. It is a sensible precaution. So, how do you feel now, Doctor?"

"Defeated. But I think this time they will have left something we can work with."

"Will tonight's episode make it difficult for you to get to sleep?"

"Death itself does not upset me. It is people who kill as casually as they break an egg who are the abominations. Kerrigan is gone, but those who killed him can and will kill again. That note revealed that these are revenge killings. The world is full of people who deal in death and destruction to get even with their enemies—blacks, whites, Christians, Muslims, Hindus, Jews. The revenge motive can so often be ascribed to people who claim some religious affiliation or other, especially when the killing is on a large scale. Have you noticed that?

"We have preventive medicine; you isolate people as soon as they start to show the first signs of infectious diseases. Why don't we find a nice large island somewhere and put all the people on it who promote, or provoke, violence."

"Because, my dear Doctor, it would put at least a third of the people working in the overdeveloped countries out of a job and cut heavily into the dividends of those who hold shares in the very profitable armaments industries. Communist or capitalist, they are all the same, they are delighted to sell us arms with which we can kill each other. *Bonsoir, mon ami, dormez bien* . . . and next time better luck with the occasion when 'they' try to kill one of 'them.'"

Quarshie put the telephone down and walked to the open-air dance floor, where he drank a lot of beer and listened to Michel sing. The beer relaxed his tensions, and the beat, which came from the drummers and the guitarists, spoke to his African soul and told him that he was connected by their pulse to roots that were deep in the past. It underlined the fact that the worries and anxieties of the moment were just that, and the moment was too brief to leave any mark.

Michel's singing comforted him, too. He showed such elegant and effortless control over the huge spectrum of rhythm, tone, harmony, counterpoint and all other aspects of music-making that he convinced Quarshie that there was more than an element of original inspiration behind life itself.

Thanks to these small insights, he later slept peacefully through the noisy murder and mayhem of a particularly vicious Hollywood movie as well as a night of shunting in which the diesel locomotive drove freight cars rolling down the tracks to fetch up against others and set off metallic chains of sound that rippled further and further away as the strings of cars in gentle collision got longer and longer.

SEVEN

They are sending a lamb to attack a lion.

It was Arrani who had named their base Alamut. He had taken the name from the history of the Ismaili Assassins. Alamut had been the name of a valley in Persia where their leader had built a castle, and the fanatical Assassins had been as fatal to their enemies as the deadliest of snakes. Besides being Ismailis they were Fatamids, a sect opposed to the Sunnis. The Fatamids claimed descent from Fatima, the murdered daughter of Muhammad. So murder was a part of the Assassins' heritage, which they passed on to the Sunnis more liberally than their victims appreciated.

Now, as dawn was breaking, Arrani climbed to a small ledge high up on one of the peaks above the base to say his prayers and to meditate.

As the sun came burning harshly up out of the sandy horizon he turned more or less towards it and precisely towards Mecca.

His prayers took him twenty minutes, by which time the sunlight already lay on his skin in an invisible layer of sulphurous heat, and he moved back into a corner where, he knew, the shade would linger for over an hour.

Though he had asked with great sincerity in his prayers for guidance, he felt that he was still badly in need of help because the previous night had loosened the knot that had, until then, kept him tied closely to the Big M and to Kali. It was directly linked to the premise he had tried to establish in his doctoral thesis, the one that had been turned down: They were Americans. He was an African.

What had inspired him to take part in their terrorist campaign against the whites was based on a fundamentally religious feeling with its roots deep in the soil of Africa. Their commitment was rooted in soil which had been irrigated and manured by television commercials, pop groups, hamburger stands, comics, electric toothbrushes, blue jeans, *Ebony* and *Playboy*, fluorescent lighting, tawdry store fronts in black ghettos, and, above all, sensationalism fostered in every imaginable way possible.

They were all influences which the Big M and Kali could not escape, and they were totally out of place in the fierce austerity of Transniger.

He looked up and out over the wide dusty plain, which might have been a moonscape in this period of the dry season, and the insignificance of the values the Big M and Kali carried in their mental baggage appalled him.

They had all three wanted to make the white man suffer for the suffering he had caused, and was still continuing to cause, and to make certain that he could never again inflict the same kind of misery on anyone. Those objectives had seemed to make such a solid bond between them that he had hoped everything else could be ignored.

After last night he realised that his actual thesis had been more correct than even he had thought. The problem in its simplest form was that the other two were not engaged, as he was, in a jihad, but in a great big blown-right-out-of-proportion gimmick, a happening.

A vulture spotted the body, which had been dragged to the outer fringes of the camp, and came sweeping down on huge wings with its primaries spread like the widely spaced fingers on a human hand. It landed a few feet away from the dead girl, regarded her first with one eye and then with the other, and after a further pause made a tentative hop towards her. When it saw that there was no movement it took two or three determined steps, which brought it up beside the girl's thigh, and then it sank its head into the opening which stretched down the centre of her abdomen.

They were mad, Arrani decided, both the Big M and Kali.

Human sacrifices and the kind of bloodletting which had taken place had to be part of a terrible sickness.

What had started as surgery, an amputation, seemed to have turned into a crazy love of brutal and bloody destruction for its own sake.

Along with this realisation came the knowledge that he could have been the one responsible for the violence of the previous night's orgy.

He and the Big M had had a disagreement.

A celebration had been due. The arms dealer had been killed . . . almost according to plan. But . . .

The man Quarshie had been awfully close on their trail. Too close. The girls, one of them an Akhanaian who knew Quarshie from the pictures in the papers, had seen him going into the hotel as they were leaving.

There could be only one reason for his having come upon them so fast. He must have deciphered the Big M's message to the newspaper.

In the beginning the Big M's premonitory notes to the press had not seemed like a bad idea, though they had not yet paid any dividends, because the fool of an editor had not had the sense to make the connection between the notes and the murders. The Big M had called it his war of nerves, though Arrani suspected that another factor had been more important. Just before he had proposed the idea the Big M had been reading Eldridge Cleaver's books. Arrani had praised the skill and natural poetry of their style. The Big M, originally unlettered like Cleaver, had wanted to show that he could do it, too. Perhaps he had also been jealous of his, Arrani's, erudition and the admiration this earned him from Kali. At the same time, maybe it was an expression of the envy of a product of the black ghetto for another black who had had the privilege of going to a university.

Now, with Quarshie in the picture, every extra detail which was added before, during or after a kill, simply added to the possibility of a foul-up. He had made this point as soon as he had heard that Quarshie was in Fort Etienne, but the Big M had had his word game ready for the arms-dealer kill and had gone ahead with it, ignoring Arrani. So, when the girls had returned, he had offered his opinion that Quarshie had successfully decoded the message.

The Big M could never admit that he had made a mistake. A black Hercules, ridged and ruthless with muscle, it was, according to his philosophy, very simple to put things right when they went wrong. Death wiped the slate clean. There was no way, he claimed, that anyone could argue with that.

When he became angry his eyes grew wider and wider until the whites showed all round the irises. If that happened, as it had happened yesterday, it spelled danger, but never for Kali or himself. The Big M had repeated the statement several times. Both his colleagues, he had said, were a physical part of him, and no one could get so crazy as to punish his own hand or his own finger. So it had to be someone else who would suffer for them, a surrogate.

That was what the dead girl, over whom several vultures were fighting now, had become.

Another bad sign was that the Big M had made a jump back to the days when he had been with the Sultans in Chicago. Something must have happened there of which he had been ashamed, though what it had been he had never told either of them. Almost always, however, when he made a mistake his mind backtracked, though it seemed to miss the target for which he was aiming. It was as if he wanted to remember the past with the intention of clearing up some unfinished business, and then, at the last moment, he sidestepped the issue.

The jerk back to that earlier life, nonetheless, went all the way. Far enough even for the hip talk of the street gangs to come back. On these occasions he always spoke to Kali, though he made certain that Arrani was in earshot.

He had told her last evening, "You know the roughest studs in our hood were the Minors. They was the boss humbuggers. Thirteen to fifteen years old they was, and nobody ever dusted them because they had so many guns. I seen some Seniors from the Egyptian Cobras walk into them one night. It was in a grey hood and the Cobras got cut, every las' one of them. The Minors did whole lots of stuff like that, and the Man never once got to them.

"My own kid brother, Grand Master Saladin, was one of them, and I seen my mother bust him in his own room one day with six shotguns hidden in there. I don't know where he got them. But nobody ever got to messing with him. He could get down on anything at all. And slick, he could whup the game on any of the fellows, whether he Samson or sixty-two across the chest."

Arrani knew that in some way the Big M was getting at him when he talked like that. He was saying, in effect, "Look what I was doing when you were still wet behind the ears."

However, Arrani thought, the Big M probably thought he was like his kid brother, the Grand Master Saladin, a typically grandiloquent name that had probably had for the kid an almost religious, and certainly a magic, value to it.

What had happened last night had started to become a convention. Arrani knew that because it involved ceremonies connected with blood, sex and death, it was, to all the others, a profoundly serious event rather than a charade that had been worked threadbare by thousands of charlatans and false shamans.

At these demonstrations all three M's wore the same style of dress.

It was a white nylon sheet attached from behind by black bands to their throats, wrists and ankles, where it was long enough to allow them to walk freely. When they crossed their hands low enough to touch their thighs the material concealed their groins. When they stood astride and raised their arms straight out and above shoulder level they showed themselves naked and looked like great bats, or butterflies with white wings and black bodies.

During the ceremonies each of their roles was well-defined. The Big M was the Master. He commanded total obedience, total attention, and assumed the position and posture of a God. Kali became the creature with the powers of creation and destruction. There was a latent cruelty in the way she played the part: it suggested that in the everlasting battle between good and evil the latter would always be the winner.

Arrani was the "linguist." Both the others spoke through him. He was also the stage manager and among other things controlled the battery-operated tape recorder which played back a variety of performances of African drummers that they had collected as they had travelled. Some of the recordings were looped to keep repeating themselves.

The site they used for the ceremonies was some distance out in front of the rock pile. It had a hip-high slab of sandstone at its centre which was encircled by ten four-gallon cans, each filled with kerosene-saturated sand that flared smokily once it was lit.

While they were at the Alamut camp none of the girls were allowed to wear any clothes. The Big M had decreed that there had to be a clear line of separation between the rank and file and the officers if proper discipline was to be maintained. Besides, he had claimed, the women felt more vulnerable when they were in the presence of males who were clothed. He had added this observation after he had told Arrani that from the women's point of view it was common knowledge that, in a number of traditional rites and cults, the women went naked. And when Arrani had corrected him and told him that the females who went naked on such occasions were prepubescents, the Big M had said, "Well, in fact, between us men, the reason I like them that way is for my own pleasure. They shouldn't be ashamed to show their Master all they've got, now should they?"

Last night's ceremony had started, as these functions always had, with a dose all round of amphetamines, and there was a fixed rite associated even with this simple prelude.

Each girl had to approach the Master and ask for "a breath of the greater life." Then, with her lips she took from between the Master's teeth an amphetamine tablet, and he closed his lips over hers as if he were breathing the drug into her. After the girl had taken the pill and was holding it in her mouth, the Big M took a mouthful of water and again, lips to lips, passed the water to her to wash the pill down her throat.

After they had all received their pills, Arrani started the tape recorder and the girls danced in a lazy way until the "magic" of the pills took effect. As they felt their excitement rising they moved into a straight line facing the rock, still stamping their feet and rolling their hips.

When they were formed up in single rank the Master, like a commanding officer inspecting his troops, walked slowly down the line running his eyes over each girl from her face down to her gyrating pelvis and back again.

Last night, when he had reached Broad Tail, she had flashed her wide grin at him.

The Master had frowned and had slapped her face so hard with his open hand that he had knocked her off her feet. Bewildered and uncertain, she had remained seated where she had fallen.

To Arrani, who always walked behind him like a platoon commander, the Master had said, "Tell her to stand up." His tone of voice was tight with anger.

She did as she was told but with a glint of fear in her eyes.

The Big M knocked her down a second time.

It was at this point, as he had helped the girl to her feet again, that Arrani became disconnected from the ritual.

As the Master moved on to the next girl Arrani knew that he was facing a moment of truth but was unable to make up his mind what he should do.

In the time left to him before the next phase he had found it difficult to think clearly or to come to a conclusion and he had failed to do either.

The Big M had continued with the usual order of the ritual, leaping agilely onto the rock beside Kali to address the girls from there.

Arrani reduced the volume of the drumming from the tape recorder, and as he proclaimed the Master's words, which were spoken to him in English in a normal conversational tone, he could see that Broad Tail was frightened.

The phrases which Arrani had had to repeat in the beginning were familiar: "Another white man has paid the price for the impurities he inherited with his white skin"; "our sisters have served us and our people well"; "since they have taken life our two sisters and I will perform the act which creates it, giving the world black men to replace white ones. Our union will have the blessing of Kali, the goddess of destruction and re-creation."

The main foreseeable difference at this point had been the fact that the sex ritual would have to be performed twice. Usually only one girl at a time was engaged in a kill.

It was during his speech, however, that the Big M introduced his first divergence from the routine.

"You will have heard," the Master pronounced, "from our two sisters that a traitor to the black cause has been enlisted to try to stop our progress towards our goal. They are sending a lamb to attack a lion. What does a lion do when it sees a lamb? It kills it and eats it.

"This lamb's carcass will be the start of a feast, for immediately afterwards we shall complete the number of deaths that will be needed to open the first of the seven gates to Gahennam. Since there are nineteen guardians around the first gate, nineteen whites will have to be killed. Thereafter, for each gate the number of dead that will be needed to pay the blood price will be the number of the dead for the previous gate multiplied by itself. Thus for the first gate nineteen will die. For the second, nineteen times nineteen will be the number. That is three hundred and sixty-one. For the third gate it will be three hundred and sixty-one times three hundred and sixty-one. That will be one hundred and thirty thousand, three hundred and twenty-one. At the fourth gate the blood price will already be into the billions. Our forces, of course, will multiply as those of the whites diminish so that before we reach the seventh gate there will be no more white men left and all our people will be free. Then the black men will rule the earth."

This was the moment when, as he translated like an automaton, Arrani began to wonder about the Big M's sanity, though his words did not sound unlike those in the Koran or in the Old Testament.

The girls had jigged on as they had listened to the Master, some of them crying out, "It is the word," or, "Hear the Master," though Arrani suspected that they were responding to the tones of his voice more than to the meaning of the words.

"But we must open the first gate before we look beyond it, and so thirteen more must die. That is what is written in the Book which tells us of our destiny and the destiny of our people.

"So, my sisters, the word is that the first to die must be the black traitor. Then to the thirteen who must follow him we shall say, as the Book says, 'Enter ye into the fire with the Djinns and to replace those whom ye consigned there.' And we shall say, 'Taste ye therefore the torment for that which ye have done.' And the thirteen will enter into the fire together and taste the torment on one and the same night."

It was revivalist stuff and the first time the Big M had used it.

Perhaps it would make sense to get this phase of the operation over and done with, now that Quarshie was on the scene, and then fade west or, perhaps, east towards Uganda. So, if the Big M had gone crazy, maybe it was "crazy like a fox."

To him, Arrani, had fallen the task of selecting the targets. It had been his job because he was locally born and could therefore blend into the background, bring in intelligence, determine the behaviour of the targets, plan the actual methods to be used for each kill, and brief and train each respective killer.

There had been a number of criteria governing the selection of the targets. The most important were that an attack could be carried out successfully, that the victims should come from as wide a range of nationalities as possible so that the operation could be seen as an attack on all white men, and that the assassinations should appear to be random and without logic so that no white in Fort Etienne could feel safe. It had also been his job, once a week, to drive those girls, who had duties to undertake in preparation for their assignments, to Fort Etienne. To avoid causing comment he usually dropped them off and picked them up, before dawn and after dark, at a convenient location just short of the outskirts of the town.

Following his declaration about the opening of the first gate to Gahennam, the Big M had returned to the usual pattern of the ritual and had called forward the two girls who had taken part in the last murder and in front of everyone had taken each of them in turn on the rock.

After that, the Master had called Broad Tail forward and had told her to kneel facing Kali, the woman who might once have been a gospel singer, and to close her eyes and lift her chin. He had then "breathed" a lump of sugar, which was well-saturated with lysergic acid, into her mouth. Then he had waved to his linguist to increase the volume of the drumming to the maximum the machine could produce.

It had been clear that the girl had soon lost all sense or orientation. She became a statue, naked, motionless, with even her eyes turned to stone.

The rest of the girls now came to dance frenetically around the rock, but Broad Tail continued to remain quite still.

After a little while the Big M had cut her right across the chest, just below the collarbone and blood had run down to coat her breasts with what appeared to be a high gloss paint.

She had continued to remain motionless.

Finally Kali and the Big M had completed the sacrifice. Kali had come from behind the girl with a garrotte while the Master, with the tip of his knife, had drawn one swift stroke from below the cord of the garrotte down the centre of her body, driving the knife deeply into the flesh below the girl's rib cage and continuing it down to her groin.

She had been left like that, arched back over her own heels as the others danced around her until the sky had begun to show the first faint traces of dawn.

Then the tape recorder had been stopped.

Each girl had been called forward and blessed by the Master in the name of Africa and all men with black skins.

Broad Tail's body had been dragged out to the edge of the camp and left there.

The Big M and Kali had gone to their cave.

And Arrani, the linguist, had climbed alone to his high platform near the summit of the rocks.

Reviewing the whole performance now, Arrani thought that they were close to the end of one phase and the beginning of a new one.

The jihad was not, of course, completed—not even the first phase of it—until the Big M had opened his first door.

After that, he decided, the pattern of the operation would have to change. That would be if he was going to stay with the two Americans.

There was no doubt that they needed him. He was more important to them than any passport. They were strangers in Africa. Without him they would be incapable of taking any action at all.

If the Big M was serious about increasing what he sometimes called "the body count," they would have to rethink their strategy. *He* would have to rethink their strategy. The Big M might be the tactical planner and also the leader because of his charisma, but he, Arrani, would have to plan the long-term future of their programme if they stayed in Africa. And the programme would have to be something closer to an urban guerilla movement, though they might start mopping up the few whites who lived outside the cities first. Whatever they did, the force they used would have to include men and women.

In the distance he heard the Big M's voice calling him, "Hey, Arrani, come on down. We got to eat, brother. Then we have to work on the logistics for the big one."

Arrani took a deep breath, stood up and moved into a patch of sun. There, his glasses flashing, he spread his arms wide and bared his lean body to the early morning fire of the sun and swore to Mother Africa that he had only just made a beginning and that he would, in the future, deserve better of her than he had so far. Then he picked his way carefully down the steep hillside to rejoin the others.

EIGHT

. . . a murderess who had just been foiled in her second attempt to kill . . .

Quarshie put down his book and put out the light. It was unusual for him to read in bed, but then it was unusual for him to be in bed without Mrs. Quarshie beside him.

He missed her.

He turned his mind to the book he had been reading. "Whether produced by what is called 'hypnosis' or what others prefer to see as simple 'suggestion,' the fact remains that all the bodily functions which are normally operated by the autonomic nervous system, over which we have no conscious control, are amenable to outside influences. Whatever the process may be, it has enormous biological significance and gives us our first direct contact with the elusive conscious."

He had seen many cures effected by witch doctors, and there could be little doubt that they had been achieved by "hypnosis" or "suggestion." Because he had been reading in English he was thinking in English, and it annoyed him that he had had to use the expression "witch doctor," because it had such a bad connotation in that language. Whites counted witch doctors, all too often, as evil men when, in fact, they were doctors who worked *against* witchcraft, evil and sickness.

Then his mind drifted to Mamadou's efforts to establish some firm evidence in relation to the murder at the Hotel Independence.

Both the girls had been described by people who saw them. One of them had been established as an Anglophone and therefore probably an Akhanaian.

The receptionist, who had booked the room to the arms salesman, was in police custody because he had not required the man to fill out the regular registration form.

The porter at the gate had told Mamadou that the girls had left just after Mamadou and Quarshie had arrived. One of the girls had been wearing a bright-red dress, and the other a green one.

The police had discovered enough fingerprints in the room to open a new registry, and dermatoglyphics had also been found of the women's feet. These might, in the end, prove more valuable than the fingerprints because the floor of the bedroom had been freshly waxed the previous morning. The most interesting feature of the footprints was the fact that one of the set had been found inside the hanging wardrobe—it had been Mamadou's idea to check in there—and the woman had actually been squatting on top of the three shallow drawers which formed the bottom of the closet. This had led Mamadou to search for anyone who might have let one of the girls into the room with a passkey. Everyone had denied being involved, so Mamadou had had soleprints made of the two night-duty chambermaids and had found that one of them had actually walked to the door of the closet. Thereafter it had not required a great deal of pressure to force her to admit that she had, indeed, let the girl in the green dress into the room and had received a sizable "dash" for her help.

So Quarshie's assumption that the man had been attacked from behind appeared to have been vindicated.

But no one had seen the girls after they had left the hotel. They had vanished into the night.

Both witnesses who had seen the girls leaving had stated that they looked happy and excited rather than anxious.

So . . . ? Quarshie wondered, what could he deduce from this evidence that was new? The garrotte had been used as usual. It was the first American who had been murdered. In fact, each victim, so far, had been of a different nationality.

One feature was new and would alter the character of his investigations very considerably: the murder had been committed by women. Perhaps this might have been true of all the murders. If it was, then it made it easier for the would-be killers to approach their victims, for no one expected a woman to kill by physical violence. A female killer usually used poison.

Thus a woman could have approached the boy in the garden as he talked to his parrot without arousing his suspicions. The Swiss could have walked past a woman on the pathway to his hut without giving her a second glance. The Russian could have been lured into his garden by a woman who claimed to be carrying a message or was pretending to be a prostitute.

The killer on the bus? A little shiver ran down Quarshie's spine. He had not been looking for a murderer amongst the women, though he had looked at them all and could even now, he thought, remember most of their faces.

He was beginning to feel sleepy. At a low level of resolution, and therefore of attention, it crossed his mind that he had seen the back view of two women, one middle-aged and heavy-set, one much younger, entering the room next to his earlier in the evening.

Michel was singing.

It would have been nice to put out his hand and draw Mrs. Quarshie towards him. Just to hear her protest and then surrender herself happily to him.

The action at the cinema was evidently taking place in a railway train, because the soporific sound of steel wheels on old-fashioned, unwelded rails ticked away steadily on the warm night air, while the real railway lines on the opposite side of the building were unusually quiet.

And then he was back walking down the gangway of the bus, looking at the faces on each side of him. Perhaps there was a girl . . . perhaps there had been a girl . . .

He fell asleep. Only to be wakened violently by somebody banging on the door of his room.

He had no idea what time it was. It must have been much later he thought, because the cinema was silent, though the dance band was still playing.

A woman's voice called softly and urgently, "Doctor Quarshie. Doctor Quarshie."

He got up, wearing an African cloth, his normal night apparel, around his hips and opened the door to find himself looking, in the light from the naked bulb on the ceiling of the verandah, at a large-bosomed woman who said, with an American accent, "Oh, forgive me, Doctor, for waking you up like this. You are a medical doctor, aren't you?" The thought crossed his mind that he had not seen her on the bus. He was still no more than half awake.

"Yes, yes, I am a medical doctor."

"I am so relieved, believe me. I didn't know what to do or where to go. You see, I have a little boy who is really awfully sick. Really awfully, awfully sick."

Quarshie came instantly fully awake as he felt something touch him lightly on the forehead and the end of his nose, and in a lightning movement he put both his hands up on each side of his neck so that his ears came down between his fingers. At the same moment that the garrotte came viciously tight around his neck he kicked the door shut in the fat woman's face.

As he turned in the dark he sensed rather than saw, or heard, someone behind him. By tearing the skin off the backs of his hands he got them free of the garrotte and threw his weight against the closing bathroom door as the intruder tried to escape. Forcing the door open he felt for the light switch and flicked it on.

He saw that his assailant was a young woman, and instantly he knew that *she* had been on the bus.

She was trapped. The whites of her eyes were enormous and she was panting.

The wall between his bathroom and the one next door was no more than an eight-foot-high partition. She must have used a chair or table on the other side that would enable her to climb over the top and drop down into his bathroom.

The girl backed to a corner and sank to the floor.

The voice with the American accent called across from the other side of the partition, "Did you get him, honey?"

Quarshie's mind would not work quickly enough. He had one of the two would-be assassins but could think of no way of capturing them both. If he made any move he was afraid he might end up with neither of them.

The girl called back softly, but desperately, "I didn't get him, I didn't get him. He's here now."

Quarshie could feel that the woman next door was suffering something like the same indecision.

Both he and the girl waited for the woman's reaction.

It came after several moments, when they heard the outside door of the further room close and the woman's quick footsteps fading away down the wooden floor of the verandah.

Her action broke the spell.

The girl seemed to shrink into herself.

Quarshie reached down and caught her by one wrist. She bit his hand and he slapped her face vigorously with the other one.

She let her head fall forward and she started to cry.

He said, "If you bite me again I'll use this garrotte on you."

She replied between sobs, "Use it. I failed. Use it."

"You did not fail on the bus."

Evidently she did not hear what he said.

She was not a beautiful girl, nor was she ugly. She was the kind of girl who, depending on mood and circumstances, could look either.

At the moment, a murderess who had just been foiled in her second attempt to kill, she looked unexpectedly pathetic.

Quarshie wished he had had Mrs. Quarshie with him. She would have known how to deal with this kind of situation better than he did.

"What is your name?" he asked.

"You were too tall. I could not . . ."

"You could not get the thing over my head without touching my face. How many other people have you killed besides the man on the bus?"

This time she raised her tear-streaked face to look at him with an expression of surprise on it, but she did not make any comment.

"Was he the only one?"

She nodded.

"And who was that woman?"

"Kali."

"Who?"

The girl shook her head.

"But there are other girls who kill people with a garrotte?"

No answer.

"And you were chosen because you saw me on the bus?"

A nod.

"Get up off the floor."

The girl did not move.

"If you don't get up I will give you a needle that will put you to sleep. When you wake up you won't know where you are or what has happened to you."

"I don't believe you have a needle which will do that." But she got up and walked past him into the bedroom. She moved towards the door onto the verandah, but he caught her by a handful of hair, not savagely, just to restrain her.

She allowed herself to be guided towards the bed without struggling.

Still holding her hair, with his hand flat on the top of her head, he turned her so that she had her back to him. He took off the garrotte, which was still around his neck, with his free hand.

"Put your hands behind you."

She made no movement.

He tightened his hold of her hair and repeated his order.

Still she made no movement.

He pulled her head back hard enough to make her open her mouth and whimper.

"Put your hands behind you."

Still no movement, but tears again.

Feeling a monster, Quarshie pushed her head forwards until she fell face downwards on the bed.

With a quick movement and facing her feet, he fought with her briefly to get the cord of the garrotte around her wrists and knotted it firmly.

Then he went into the bathroom and took the leather strap he kept around his doctor's bag, returned with it and stood looking down at her.

She turned her head sideways to watch him but made no move or sound.

He strapped her ankles together, turned her over, and while he was lifting her into a sitting position she tried to bite his shoulder. He grinned at her. "You're as vicious as a little barracuda and have as much fight in you. I doubt that even if I beat you I could make you talk, so I am going to have to get another kind of help."

He caught a glint of devilishness in her eyes.

She lifted her knees and he saw that she had wetted his bed.

And he found that he had to laugh.

"You're a nasty little animal," he told her.

"You've made me very frightened. You would not have let me go outside, would you?"

He shrugged and started to dress, pulling on a shirt and a pair of trousers and went towards the door. Then as an afterthought he went back to his doctor's bag, took out a wide roll of adhesive tape and stretched a section of it across her mouth.

"I would not want you disturbing other guests in the hotel. Though if they have learned to sleep through the noise from the trains, the cinema and the band, I don't suppose you could disturb them even if you screamed your head off. I shall not be long."

Walking barefooted along the verandah outside, he unexpectedly felt elated. He had not only escaped murder but had caught one of the murderers.

He went down the outside staircase to the dance floor where the band was still playing for a few couples, though he saw from his watch that it was almost four o'clock.

Michel seemed half asleep, as if he had moved into the music itself.

When the number was finished, Quarshie walked up onto the bandstand and as Michel moved towards him he told him, "I need your help. It's urgent." Michel spoke briefly to the trumpeter and then followed Quarshie back to his room.

Quarshie unlocked the door and saw that the bed was empty.

The girl was standing, balanced rather precariously on her strapped feet, in a corner of the room.

"She tried to kill me," Quarshie told Michel as he removed the tape from her mouth. To her he said, "What are you doing over here?"

"It was very uncomfortable in the bed," she replied sullenly.

"First she tries to garrotte me, then she wets my bed, now she complains that she has made it uncomfortable."

Ignoring Quarshie, she asked, "Who is this white nigger?"

Quarshie told Michel, "She was helped by another woman who got away. Can you tell me anything about them?"

The girl repeated, "Who is this man? I don't know him. How can he know anything about me?"

Michel switched on the small bedside lamp and switched off the one which glared from the centre of the ceiling. Then he walked over to the girl and took a small gold chain from her which she was wearing around her neck.

"What are you going to do?" It was the first time Quarshie had heard anxiety in her voice rather than defiance or fear.

Michel sat down facing her, holding the gold chain lightly in one hand.

"What is he doing?" the girl demanded again. "I fear him. He is a soul eater."

After a while Michel said, "There is a house. It has two floors, and upstairs the verandah is closed in with mosquito netting. The woodwork of the house is painted brown. There is a thin yellow dog with white feet which guards it. This you have on your mind. This you remember."

Unwillingly the girl said, "It is my father's house."

"The palm trees are not like the ones here. They are taller and they bend in a strong wind."

"It blows every day from the sea," the girl added. The words seemed to force themselves out of her and she shrank back against the wall.

Quarshie glanced from the albino to the girl and back again, and knew that their minds had locked together in some way and that he was only a spectator.

"Not long ago a woman died. No, she was killed and her body was given to the vultures. This also is on your mind."

"How do you know?" She sat without blinking, her eyes fixed on Michel's face. "How do you know?"

Quarshie felt as if Michel was tightening something down with a spanner, gaining more and more power with each pronouncement.

"You have also in your mind a voice which told you that many people will die, and the commands of that voice are such that you must obey them."

"When will these people die?" The question came from Quarshie.

"Tomorrow night." The girl did not seem to be aware of Quarshie, nor did she register any difference between his voice and Michel's.

"Who will do the killing?" Quarshie spoke very softly, and to his surprise the answer came from Michel.

"Women. My head hurts." He closed his eyes and let his head fall back.

Quarshie knelt beside the albino so that his head rested on the Doctor's shoulder. Michel looked as if he was asleep, and Quarshie remembered that he had been singing all evening.

The girl watched them both.

"What is your name?" Quarshie asked her.

"Amoa, sir." She looked as if she was coming out of shock.

"What else can you tell me about the people who will be killed tomorrow night?"

"Nothing. I haven't told you anything. *He* told you. How does he know?"

Quarshie got up and took the pillow and put it on the mat alongside the bed. He also took a light flannel sheet which was folded across the end of the bed. Then he lifted Michel off the chair, laid him on the mat with his head on the pillow, and covered him with the sheet.

When he saw that Michel did not move and was, in fact, asleep, he moved the chair he had been sitting on so that he could watch Amoa and Michel at the same time.

"That American woman, Kali, is the boss, isn't she? And the voice which told you that many people would die was her voice, wasn't it?"

The girl shrugged.

"Perhaps she isn't the boss. Perhaps there is a man. Is there?"

Amoa shook her head. "You had better ask him when he wakes up."

"Why did you want to kill me? You have not killed any black people before."

"You are a traitor."

"To whom?"

"To Africa. Africa will only be free when all the white people everywhere are dead."

"So that is what he says?"

"Yes."

"Many times?"

"Many times."

"Does he speak in English?"

"To the linguist, he . . ." She realised that she had been trapped and held her tongue.

"So the linguist must speak English, too. That's two men and one woman."

"I did not say that."

Quarshie sighed.

"As soon as Michel wakes up," he said, "he will go and fetch the police. They will continue with this questioning, perhaps all day and all night. They won't stop until you tell them all that they want to know. They will take your clothes away, too, because they will want to examine them. They will, perhaps, have dust on them, which will tell us where you have been living and therefore where to look for the others. There is enough evidence now to have you charged with attempted murder and suspicion of murder. Here, you know, it is not like Akhana. There you are innocent until you are proved guilty. Here, if the examining magistrate decides that you may be guilty, you are held until you can prove your innocence. You will probably save yourself a lot of unhappiness if you tell me everything you know."

"I can't tell you or them anything. I failed. If I go back to . . . If I go back I shall deserve to be executed."

"That is what happens to the other girls when they fail, is it? They are executed."

"None of them have failed. I am the first."

"And we shall get them all, whether you talk or not. The two men and that American woman. Also, of course, all those who work for them. And they will guess that you talked and told us everything. So you have nothing to lose by talking. If you answer my questions I can ask them to be merciful to you—I, whom you tried to kill—and they are bound to listen to me."

She started to cry again, but she said nothing.

"Actually," Quarshie told her, "I am sorry for you. You are being used by people who are cleverer than you are. You think I have been trying to trick you. *They* tricked you."

Michel stirred, opened his eyes and after a moment sat up.

Quarshie helped him to his feet and they walked out onto the verandah together.

"Did I help?" he wanted to know.

"Yes, very much."

"But this is not the end yet."

"You know it isn't."

"What should I do now?"

"Go and see Mamadou. You may have to wait for him to finish saying his prayers. Then get him to bring a police car to take this girl away. After that, go to bed . . . and thank you, friend."

"Thank me when I can really help you. That girl is sick from what others have done to her. They are people who are full of a plague themselves and spread it to other people. Even to children, like that one." He gestured with his head towards the bedroom.

Quarshie gave Michel some money and said, "Take a taxi and tell Mamadou to hurry. With your help and his, this will all be over quite soon."

Michel said, "Yes, sir." And departed.

Beyond the tall trees the sky was beginning to pale.

A cicada chirped tentatively, chirped again with a little more certainty, and finally once again before it set up a steady, high-pitched vibration that was almost a whistle.

Quarshie wondered if it was the one which had sat on his knee in the bath.

In his room Amoa was sitting on the floor bent forward so that her tears fell into the lap of her skirt.

Quarshie took her by the elbow and told her to lay down on the mat which had been vacated by Michel.

Miserably, in a voice that was little more than a whisper, she said, "I wanted to do something good. We have to get rid of all the whites. They don't think that there is a place for us in the world, or that we should be alive. They beat us and kill us when we live amongst them. So why should we not kill them when they come to our countries? The little one, Arrani, the linguist, told me much of the history, and he had a book with things cut from newspapers in it and gave it to me to read. To the whites we are not people like they are. We smell, we are dirty, we are stupid. Lots of people in those newspapers said things like that. So why should they be free to come here when they feel like that?"

Quarshie said, "Lie down and rest."

"You know these things, too. Don't you?"

"Everybody knows them. But you do not cure a disease by killing everyone who suffers from it. Lie down, child. Revenge is a *cul de sac* or worse, a vicious circle." The girl did as she was told, and Quarshie covered her with the sheet as he had covered Michel.

Feeling less elated than he had earlier, Quarshie went and sat on a chair to wait for the police.

The girl had stopped crying and presently she turned her head towards him and told him, "I'm sorry I wet your bed, sir."

Quarshie smiled at her and said, "Never mind. As a doctor, I can tell you that it is something which happens to people sometimes when they are frightened. Only they don't enjoy it like you did."

With a shadow of a smile showing through her tears, Amoa said, "Yes, I did enjoy it. Not everyone is able to do something like that to the famous Doctor Quarshie."

NINE

The killing of this devil is the beginning of bliss.

Sitting with Quarshie, in comfortable armchairs in the General's office were the General, himself, his Chef de Cabinet, and Mamadou.

The office was on the second floor, and when Quarshie glanced through the window, which was behind the General, he could see a middle-aged woman following a footpath outside the walls of the Residence. She was bearing a tremendous load of firewood, and instead of carrying it on her head she carried it on her back in a sling which led from her forehead down over her shoulders. She had to lean forward into the sling, which meant that almost all the weight was carried against the forward thrust of her neck. A man, probably her husband, rode well back over the rump of a donkey, just behind her.

In the distance some vultures wheeled high in the sky like a great astral mobile over a garbage dump on the further side of the river. Just beyond the man and the woman, a small sand-devil tried to work up enough energy to start its whirling-dervish dance, but collapsed before it could achieve enough momentum.

"Should I say that you were lucky, my friend?" asked the General.

"I was, sir. I was also lucky to get the girl to talk as much as she did." Quarshie was keeping Michel's special gifts to himself, partly out of fear that the others would not be prepared to risk as much as he had on their effectiveness, partly to save the young man from being asked to demonstrate his talents, and partly because, if they became known, Michel might also become a target for the assassins. "Of course," he continued, "Amoa is busy now denying that she told me anything. She spoke while she was suffering from the shock of her failure, discovery and capture."

"So you think there are Americans behind these revenge killings?" The question came from the Chef de Cabinet. In his usual quiet tone of voice he added, "They have from fifteen to twenty murders a day over there. We seldom have that many in a year. Savages . . . isn't that what they used to call us? And they encourage aggression. When you are an aggressive salesman, administrator, or athlete, you are an object of admiration." He spoke from several years' experience as the representative of Transniger at the United Nations. During that time he had travelled around the country, read the local tabloids and breathed the atmosphere of violence which seeped, like fumes from a sewer, through some sections of the big cities and could even be found in some much smaller, rural towns.

"A corrupt society," the General said, "with great power, which they quite often use to cure that corruption. They have the biggest crime establishment in the world, are the greatest crusaders for truth and liberty, and elect into political power some of the crookedest men they can find. Fortunately, there are enough honest Americans to maintain some sort of balance, though the situation gets pretty precarious sometimes. We are lucky here, because the United States Ambassador is not only an able and pleasant man but a scholar."

"Though his scholarship relates to the history of human migrations in the Pacific. So they sent him to a country on the fringe of the Sahara," added the Chef de Cabinet. And then, changing the subject, he said, "Since you phoned, Doctor, His Excellency and I have been preparing a list of precautions we are going to take. I hope the information from the girl is reliable, because if it is not it is going to look like we are in something of a panic. We are sending out notices to all the ambassadors, alerting them to the facts and advising them to take advantage of the protective measures we are offering. These include six military guards per household who will be on twenty-four-hour duty, and mobile squads of police under officers or senior N.C.O.'s who can be called into action through an emergency telephone number. We are advising those expatriates who don't have telephones to move in with the ones who do. Those who live in isolated areas are getting larger squads of soldiers to guard them, or are being advised to move to safer locations. We are setting up roadblocks all around the city and have given the police the right to search all incoming travellers. They are to look particularly for people carrying lengths of nylon line. Anyone found with them will be taken in for questioning. Finally, all whites have been advised of the Quarshie method of protecting themselves against being strangled. How are your hands, by the way?"

Quarshie held his hands up to show that the knuckles on both of them were covered with sticking plasters.

"Nothing serious," he said. "Lost a certain amount of skin, that's all."

"Do you have anything to add?" the General asked.

Quarshie thought for a moment and then replied, "We have no solid evidence that men will not be used as killers. If they were really clever they might use women to begin with and then, when we were concentrating on looking for women, switch to men. Although it would be my bet that the two men the girl mentioned, and that female who acted as a decoy, are the leaders." Quarshie suddenly remembered Mamadou's trick of being able to remember obscure pieces of information and said to his assistant, "She named one of the men as Arrani . . . does that mean anything to you? I mean the name 'Arrani'?"

Mamadou looked nervously from one to the other of the three men facing him.

"Take your time, my son," the General said. "Go into the inner office where we won't distract you and let that phenomenal memory of yours get to work."

When the door closed behind Mamadou, Quarshie said, "He's a fine young man. I am happy you made him my assistant."

"It was His Excellency's suggestion." The Chef de Cabinet was perhaps trying to avoid any suggestion of nepotism, Quarshie thought, but the General happily took the credit. "I've known him since he was a child and played with my children," the old man told Quarshie. "His mind always worked on a different plane from theirs. We don't have so many talented people here that we can afford to waste them. They need to be cultivated with as much intelligence as we can muster and pushed forward with as much vigour as they can tolerate. His work with you will certainly help his development. I detect an inclination in him to become a recluse, and I am hoping that being involved with you in this project will make him realize how much we need his talents."

"If it does not kill him or get him killed." Quarshie thought he detected now a suggestion that there might have been some disagreement between the General and his aide over the appointment.

"That is a risk that all leaders, or those who train to be leaders, must accept." And with a smile he added, "As the Doctor's recent experience has just demonstrated. One learns to live with it, doesn't one, my friend?"

Mamadou came back into the room.

"Well?" the General said.

"Yes, sir. Bu Tahir Arrani . . . there are many Arranis, of course, but Bu Tahir was a man who pretended to be a Sufi. He was the first man to kill for the Assassins. Hassan ben Sabbah, their leader, when he heard that Arrani had killed the Assassins' worst enemy, said, 'The killing of this devil is the beginning of bliss.' I think that fits the picture, doesn't it, sir?" he said, turning to Quarshie.

"Very good, Mamadou. And you said the name of the Assassins' leader was Hassan?"

"Yes, sir."

"Then let's try another supposition. Arrani and the linguist the girl talked about could be one and the same person, and therefore it could be possible that the boss might call himself Hassan, since a linguist has to serve a Chief. Of course it is a long shot, but one that is worth trying on the girl. It might make her think that we know more than we do and that therefore she might as well tell us the rest."

"Don't you think a whip might do that more effectively?" The question came from the Chef de Cabinet.

Quarshie shook his head. "Torture is an unreliable way of getting information, as the French found out in Algeria. With a few people it even makes them more obstinate. It is not a question of courage but of something almost biological that is associated with hate. If you hurt me badly it makes me hate you so much that it gives me the strength to resist you. Alternatively, the victim can surrender completely and tell everything and more, making up things when he runs out of the truth. The girl does not have a very formidable intelligence. Before long we shall have got most of the things out of her that we want to know. Besides . . ."

"Yes, my friend," the General prompted him, "besides . . ."

"The girl is a tool, sir. One that has been put out of action. From the beginning she has not known what she was really doing. Others have followed false prophets because they wanted to do what they thought was the right thing. They and she were and are without the intellectual resources to evaluate their 'saviour.'" He paused, then added, "Even if this attack which we anticipate does not come off this evening, I think you should continue with the precautions until the emergency is over. The fact that the diligent efforts of the police have failed to locate the base from which these assassins are operating suggests that they must be located well off the beaten track, somewhere out in the savannah maybe, or north towards the desert.

To search that area I need a helicopter. I know there is only one in the country and that it belongs to the Office of the President, sir. With all the other co-operation I have received, I hardly dare to ask that it be put at my disposal."

The Chef de Cabinet raised his eyebrows and said crisply, "That is something only His Excellency can decide."

"And of course you shall have it, Doctor. No doubt you know already that my pilot is a genial young man from your country. I will order him to give you the fullest freedom in the way you choose to use it. Quite a lot of our discussion has been in military terms. This reflects a simple fact. It is that we are at war. So we must mobilise as if we are. You will command our air force, Doctor. One helicopter."

TEN

. . . the God who had brought death into the world . . .

"O.K.," said the Big M, without knowing he was echoing the General, "we treat it as a military exercise. We lost some real estate, and that has put us on the defensive. That's what the enemy will think. So the last thing he will expect is to find us on the offensive."

He had taken Kali's news that Amoa had failed surprisingly coolly. "You win some, you lose some," had been his first reaction.

"So what will they have learned from her by now?" he asked rhetorically. "And what will they do? I'll tell you. Whatever they know, they will double and maybe redouble their defences, and they will set up roadblocks into the town. What will they look for? Garrottes." He got up and went and stood in the entrance of the cave, looking out into the harsh white glare of the afternoon sunlight.

Presently he came back and stood in front of Kali and Arrani, where they were squatting on their bedrolls.

"Anyway, we shall go ahead with the schedule, but with one change. The jobs will be done knowing, from here on in, that the girls are expendable. Phase one is coming to an end, and we shall start over, for phase two, with a new formation."

Arrani nodded, surprised how close the Big M's thinking came to his on important occasions.

"You agree. Good. Then I'll tell you what we'll do. We'll go in through the back door. They won't expect us to come in down the river. You, Brother Arrani, will be the only one in the truck. By yourself you won't arouse any suspicions. You don't need to have papers except for the truck, and they're legit. Your story will be that you are going into town to pick up a load."

"And you?"

"There are some fishermen a little way up the river. They work at night with lights set up over the fishtraps. They have one big canoe with an outboard and a couple of others. I can handle an outboard. We used them on the Mekong a couple of times. When the fishermen have set their lights, they lay around and maybe sleep a little. They don't operate close to the village, because the people there throw stuff in the river, wash themselves and their clothes in it, disturb the fish. They work two miles upstream above the village. Maybe they would like some nice feminine company to help them pass the evening. You will drop all of us up near there with the truck soon after it gets dark. Maybe they too will turn out to be expendable. Of course they'll go down to Fort Etienne. Dead and in the river. We'll get there ahead of them in the boats, using the one with the outboard as a tugboat for the others. Sound O.K.?"

Arrani polished his glasses with the corner of his cloth.

"And getting back?" he asked slowly.

"There'll be just the three of us. Then we head north to that other site we found out there. We'll blow Fort Etienne before the girls make any kills, so that the people at the checkpoints won't be all uptight. We'll pick up all that we'll need from here—water, food, artillery—and then we fade. Sit out there for a while, make a new set of plans. If we see any signs that anyone found this place while we were gone, we'll come in very slowly and carefully and we'll cache the sack of money down the trail before we go. On the way back we'll pick up the money first, and if we get suspicious we'll think again. Maybe head for the Cameroons. Right?"

"Are you scared of Quarshie?" Kali asked.

"Scared ain't the right word, sister. Just cautious. He has the big guns, doesn't he? Army, police, transportation . . . you name it, he's got it. I don't fight out of my class, baby. If you was alone and had the power to become invisible and the enemy was after you with everything, wouldn't you touch that 'fade me out' button? I sure as hell would and fast."

"Crazy like a fox," Arrani told himself again.

Kelolo, besides being a most successful fisherman, was widely known for his skill as a storyteller.

It had been a long day: he and the other two men from the village had had to repair the nets, because the previous night a hippopotamus had blundered into them.

Now, with the trap reset and the torches burning to attract the fish, he was rewarding his companions, as they sat around a small fire they had used to bake some yams, with a traditional tale about three strangers who had once visited their village.

It was too early for the moon to have risen, so the only light came from the silvery radiance of the stars.

With Kelolo's detailed descriptions the other fishermen were sure that the events Kelolo recounted had actually happened and that the story must be true.

The three men who came visiting the village, in Kelolo's story, told the village headman that they were reincarnations of God the creator, the God who governed sickness and the God who had brought death into the world.

When the first God introduced himself the old village headman got very angry and said, "Take yourself off. We have no time for you here. For, at the same time that you created the world, you created injustice. You made some men clever and some stupid, some women beautiful and some ugly, some children strong and some weak. Even the animals you made are unequal. One cow gives much milk and another only a little, some dogs can run very fast and have strong, sharp teeth and some have short legs and mouths so small that they can barely open them wide enough to bark. Because of these terrible blunders you made and the suffering they cause, you are quite unwelcome here. Kindly leave the village immediately."

When he learned the identity of the second stranger, the village headman grew even angrier still and told him, too, to be off. "For you are even more unjust. You also give unequal attention to men by making some blind or deaf, some impotent, and some so crippled that they cannot even mend a net. You make some women barren and others whose milk dries up too soon, some who deliver babies which die quickly and some who fall prey to women's sicknesses and then infect men with them. And you do all these evil things to just a few so that they suffer far more than all the others. So you, too, are unwelcome here. Leave us or we shall have to drive you away with sticks and stones."

It was, however, different when the God who had introduced death into the world made himself known. To him the headman said, "My friend, you are welcome, for to you all men are equal, the rich and the poor, the ruler and the slave, the swift and the slow, the white and the black, the man of wisdom and the fool. So you, my master, are welcome here."

It was questionable, of course, whether Kelolo would have told that particular tale if he had known that a big man, a stranger with bottles of gin, would visit his fishing camp quite so soon after he had finished. With the gin they poured libations to the nets and to the ancestors, and then, being pressed by the big stranger, they drank too much of it too quickly.

Later, though Kelolo and his helpers had been unaware of them, young women had come out of the shadows and had introduced all three fishermen to the last God in Kelolo's story: death.

At the hands of these young women the "master of equality" had come swiftly, surprisingly, and almost without fear.

After that, the bodies were put in the water and the Big M embarked his women in three canoes and ferried them quickly downriver, under tow, to a deserted stretch of the riverbank in Fort Etienne, where they all landed unobserved and set off in different directions.

Michel lay on his back and stared at the ceiling, which was really no more than the underside of the hut's flat mud roof. It was whitewashed and at certain times it provided him with something like a cinema screen onto which he could project visualisations of his thoughts. When these were no more than daydreams the images were cheerful ones, often related to his ambition to lead a band which would play music that he had arranged for them. It would have a sound which made it uniquely "his" band, and over and over again he heard in his mind combinations of instruments he would like to use. He longed to use a piccolo and flute in harmony to carry a theme against typically African polyrhythmic or polymetric backgrounds on all kinds of percussion instruments, traditional and Western, even adding to this section a slurred and repeated burp from a trombone.

It was too early for him yet to go to the Hotel Buffet de la Gare for work, and he was having to resist an impulse to go and find Quarshie. The Doctor filled a need in his life for an association with a strong but understanding man, a big man, maybe a man who would be his protector.

Quarshie . . . Michel's first sight of him had been like seeing a comet flashing across the night sky. Though there were billions of stars behind it, you saw only the blunt bullet nose with its great tail of glowing phosphorus, and nothing of the little prickles of light that were the stars.

Then the sensation, which he dreaded, started to come over him: his mouth went dry, he found it hard to breathe, and his limbs became taut, rigid, almost paralysed. There was no escape from it. He could not get off his bed, though he felt threatened. At a certain moment it was as if a guitar string snapped. He started to sweat, the ceiling went dark and then came alive with red-hot pinpoints of fire which rose to meet him as if they came out of the nozzle of a hose. At the same time there was a totally unfamiliar sound in his ears, though part of it seemed to be identifiable as engine noise and part of it as something close to the shriek of a high wind.

Somehow, he knew for certain that he was living ahead in the future, that his powers had been extended and that this was the most terrifying form they had ever taken.

After a moment he felt a weight on his shoulder and there was blood running down his arm. It was not *his* blood. He was sure it was not his blood.

Then there was a giddy spinning sensation and choking clouds of dust.

Finally, as if it were coming towards him through a sandstorm, he saw the body of a big man spreadeagled over a rock and there was blood shining on the smooth surface. The most terrible part of this picture was the man's head. It was spread over the rock like the head of a locust after a man has put his heel on it.

Slowly the picture faded. The ceiling became white again and he returned to his sweating, rigid body on his bed in his own room. Then, only moments later, he slipped into a short, dreamless sleep.

Doctor Janus Rykowski was a very tired man. This was not a condition brought on by overwork, although certainly he was overworked, but his fatigue was deep in his bones and in his mind.

He was a Jew but he did not feel like other Jews, especially the Hasidic Jews, amongst whom he had been brought up. Above everything else he detested narrow-mindedness, people who presumed to believe that they were God's chosen people and then reacted with cries of "discrimination" when those who were not "chosen" were intolerant.

He justified his own existence by believing that the world really needed men and women who could mend broken or malfunctioning bodies.

In Danzig, as a young man, he had worked in a state of continuous tension that had been created by the German threat to the "corridor." It so obviously invited the "appendectomy" that Herr Hitler had eventually performed.

Then Warsaw, Warsaw in the weeks between the first of August and the second of October 1944, a period that had seen the last of a succession of bitter disasters which had wracked the city during Hitler's war. Earlier there had been almost a month of hell in 1943 when the ghetto was razed and fifty-six thousand Jews were killed or taken off to concentration camps.

Afterwards the Polish underground movement had continued its operations, and broken and torn bodies were continually brought into the basement, under the rectory of the cathedral of St. John, where he had worked and slept without ever seeing the light of day.

Then someone, after the surrender of Warsaw, had given him away to the Germans. The result was Buchenwald—where he had still been able to do a little mending, only this time it was of broken minds. He continued to wear, after he was freed, a tattooed number on his forearm with a curious feeling of pride.

Then he had lived in London with other refugees, had requalified in medicine, had taken British nationality, and for a few years had lived a fairly normal life.

Cyprus, Enosis and attachment to the U.N. peacekeeping force followed the period spent in London, and again he had had the job of mending broken bodies and felt a nasty twist in his gut every time he heard a burst of gunfire.

Next had come Stanleyville, still with the U.N. forces, this time running a hospital set up to take care of troops from Ethiopia, Ghana, Morocco and Tunisia. Though the climate on the banks of the Congo had been hot, humid and unpleasant, he had enjoyed his work there, perhaps because his patients had treated him with the simple, honest respect they would have given their fathers.

Then, in his view, an iniquity had been committed by the world against Lumumba. The Doctor's attitude in the affair had been clinched after the publication of the earnest young man's last letter to his wife. It had read, "But what we have wanted for our country, the right to honourable life, to untarnished dignity, to unrestricted freedom . . . these things have never been desired on our behalf by those important officials at the U.N. in whom we put our trust and upon whom we called for help because, whether they knew it or not, they were directly or indirectly supporting the colonialism of Belgium and her friends in the West." He, himself, had been witness to the fact that there had been much truth in those words.

From there the step to Fort Etienne had been an easy one. He had found that Africans, with all their faults and shortcomings, were people whom he could love.

With all their faults . . . one of which was the way gossip spread amongst them. A story that was completely false had been started—that he had refused a man from a local tribe a blood transfusion because the only blood in the right group, in the hospital's tiny blood bank, was being saved in case a white man with blood belonging to that group needed a transfusion.

It was a story that, in an even more garbled form, had reached the Big M and Arrani.

So it followed that that evening, as the Doctor sat on his verandah, reflecting on the past over a glass of whisky and soda, he thought he heard his steward behind him and called over his shoulder, without looking around, "Nicholas, this he be the las' whisky I go take tonight. Make you go, one time, for your house."

The words "last whisky ever" would have been more appropriate, because the noose of a garrotte was dropped neatly over his head from behind. Though he fought with the cord, tearing at it with his fingers, it was only a few seconds before he was unconscious . . . a few minutes before he was dead.

For the girl who had killed him it had been simple. She had been sleeping with the Doctor's steward on and off for several months. Now the steward, the night watchman, and their master had given up their lives to her, a peasant girl, who only knew how to do one thing, to use a garrotte.

When other girls had told her how easy it was she had not believed them. Now she did.

As she had done many times before, she walked past the military guard at the entrance to the hospital along with the fifty or so visitors who were allowed in for an hour, at half past eight, to visit patients. As usual, and quite unhurriedly, she left with them.

It was much later when one of the hospital staff, coming to call the Doctor to deal with a road-accident case, had found him dead and had reported this to the police.

Commandant Pierre Courtois was military attaché at the French Embassy in Fort Etienne. He was a *colon* from Algiers and a veteran of many years' service in the French Army. He had served with the Croix de Lorraine forces in Syria during World War II. He had been in Indochina from the beginning of the fighting there, and he had also served in military intelligence in Algiers before DeGaulle sidled out of France's commitment to the colons.

Courtois was a man without scruple or pity and had been prepared to fight the Algerians, in what he saw as his native country, to the last breath in his body and the last volt in the batteries his unit used to torture the prisoners who were brought in for interrogation.

In the last analysis, however, loyalty to the Army stood higher in his code of honour than loyalty to Algeria. So he had returned to France and had been posted overseas to Bamako to take charge of the military training establishment there. After Mali achieved independence he was given the job of military attaché in Fort Etienne and was marking time there waiting to be retired.

It was a soft job but he allowed nothing to weaken his military spirit—not even his penchant for African women.

So he scrutinised the pretty girl, who came in carrying two African masks and some African brasswork, very carefully. It was widely known that he was a collector of African art. He treated it as an investment. He knew the genuine thing from the stuff made for tourists, and when he found the former he sent it in boxloads to Casablanca, where an agent arranged for its disposal at prices which often gave him close to a hundred per cent profit.

One of the masks that the girl had was good, an excellent piece; but the girl . . .

He told her in her own language to sit on the floor and wait for a moment. Then he went to the door and spoke softly in French to his steward.

After that, he came back, sat down in a chair in front of the girl and started to examine the brasses she had brought with her. When she stood up to hand him a small Ashanti gold weight he told her roughly to sit down and not to stand up again unless he told her to. However, he took the gold weight and examined it.

A moment later, two armed soldiers came in and saluted. He told them to stand on each side of the girl and to hold her arms.

Then in a leisurely way he began to search her, taking libidinous pleasure in his task. There was nothing inside the bodice of her semi-African dress, though he felt around inside it for quite a long time. Then he turned to the cloth which she wore as a skirt, raising it and lowering the briefs she wore beneath it, having the soldiers force her to open her legs so that he could search between them. Finally he finished his investigation by unwinding the roll of cloth which formed the top of her skirt, leaving this place to the last because he knew that, if his suspicions were correct, it would be there that he would find the garrotte.

The girl was whimpering but not struggling.

In a moment he held what he was looking for in his hand.

For a while he stood and stared at the girl, debating what he should do. Finally, he decided that there were too many witnesses to do what he would have liked to do, so he shrugged, went to the telephone and called the police.

He looked again at the mask and the gold weight and decided that they were two pieces which he would not send to Casablanca—not only because they had not cost him anything, so there were no expenses to be recouped, but also because they would serve as a peg upon which to hang a titillating reminiscence when he had the right audience to whom he could show off his collection.

The Goethe Institut in Fort Etienne stayed open late because of classes for students learning German. At the same time the library was well-patronised at that time of night.

Herr Faber, the elderly Director, appeared to be a fatherly figure whose appearance was betrayed every time he looked anyone directly in the eye. The look was always loaded with suspicion, particularly if the person he was looking at had a black skin.

"They shteal everytink," he told his opposite number at the British Council reading room and library one day, "the earphone from language lab, the magazines, the papers, the books, even the elegdrik light fittinks."

However, he showed less suspicion than usual when a healthy, robust African woman, who was a little older than most of the students who used the Institut said, politely, "Monsieur, I am looking for a book by Heinrich Zimmermann on postnatal care for infants. It was on one of the shelves in the reference section yesterday, but it seems to have disappeared."

"Ach," replied Herr Faber, "we will find it, I am sure. Come, we will look together."

The shelf the book would normally have occupied was in the section of the library which formed a *cul de sac*. To look on the right shelf for it, the Director had to squat on his heels, and the woman who had asked for the book stood behind him, with his head at about the level of her waist.

In this instance luck favoured Herr Faber. A young male African student, who was looking for the Director, turned the corner of the bookshelves just at the moment the woman dropped the nylon cord over Herr Faber's head. He had no difficulty in overpowering the woman. Then, twisting her arm painfully behind her back, he and the Director took her to the front door and called the security forces who were on duty just outside.

It was only after three policemen had marched her off to the police station and Herr Faber was giving his story to a fourth policeman that he discovered he was still wearing the garrotte, like a necklace, around his throat.

With hands which were now, for the first time, shaking, he took it off and thrust it at the policeman, saying, "*Aber* this is evidence, this is evidence. I do not vant it. You must take it. Ja, you must take it avay . . . take it right avay."

Michel's desire to contact Quarshie was being reflected back towards the albino by the Doctor, who was watching the activities, at the central police station, of a small group of men manning the special command post that had been set up there.

Everyone, Quarshie felt, including himself, was operating in the dark, and no one except Michel was equipped to work in such conditions. One of the police sergeants, watching Quarshie as the big man sat with his elbows on the arms of his chair and his chin in his hands, thought, "There is one man who feels he is in control"—an observation that would have brought a smile to Quarshie's lips. He had just remembered an African aphorism which stated, "A live man is happier than a dead man because he can taste the water he drinks, smell wood smoke on the wind, hear a child's laughter, and make love to a woman. But those who are dead are more powerful." And he was wondering if Michel could contact the dead and get help from them.

Whether one believed them or not, the messages, which were transmitted from the dead by African mediums, came from their ancestors and were of great practical importance. These messages might tell their kin when and where to open up new fields for planting, help them to get over disease, send them on long journeys and have a serious influence on them in many other ways. African mediums sometimes spent five years' apprenticeship before they were accepted as mediums in their own right. Did African society preserve a greater sense of interpersonal sensitivity and therefore make it easier for individuals to exchange information at an extrasensory level? Or could a medium—could Michel—really contact the ancestors and get information from them?

His speculations were interrupted by the noise of car doors being slammed and the police bringing in the first of the would-be assassins. She came from the Military Attaché's house, and while she had been frightened at first, now she was sullen and angry. The man's behaviour had convinced her, if she needed any convincing, of the Master's often repeated statement that "the only good white man is a dead one."

The girl was taken through the charge room and straight to a specially prepared cell at the back. Besides Amoa, it contained a microphone which was made up to look like a light fitting, without a bulb in it, suspended over the centre of the room. The lead from the microphone was plugged into a tape recorder, which was set in operation as soon as the girls began to talk.

The Café du Golfe de Tong King was run by a fat woman from North Vietnam. It was popular with expatriates living in Fort Etienne because the food was good, varied and reasonable in price.

For those reasons it was a regular rendezvous for two Americans when one of them, Tom Lassiter, Jr., a geologist who was doing a survey for uranium out in the northern desert area, was in town. His companion, Charles R. McKeown, was responsible for USAID in Fort Etienne and was an operations officer in the "Company," a fact which was known only to the United States Ambassador and, through their own sources, to the General and his Chef de Cabinet.

The man on the Transniger desk at the State Department in Washington had reason to believe that Lassiter could be bought, and it was important, so far as his uranium search went, that this aspect of his character should be checked out and watched.

If the circumstances had not been what they were, it was possible that these two men could have become friends. They were both well-qualified in their particular academic interests; Lassiter had his degree in geology, and McKeown had his in physics from M.I.T. They were both New Englanders, and both, at one time or another, had spent quite a lot of time sailing along the United States Atlantic seaboard. Also, they were both quite sensitive, with the result that Lassiter felt that there was some underlying motive in McKeown's friendship, and McKeown felt that Lassiter had this feeling. So they both spent too much of their time feinting and fencing for their friendship to grow as fully as it could have.

Or rather, that was the case until they spent this particular evening dining together at the Café du Golfe, to give the place its colloquial name, and the lights went out.

The total darkness which followed was unexpected by everyone except the waiter, who had been well paid to cause the lights to fuse, and two young women in African-style clothes who had been sitting at a table next to the two Americans and had swiftly and silently tried to slip garrottes over their heads.

In the dark, the one sitting furthest from her target, Lassiter, had fumbled the job and had to break away from his grasp, leaving him with her cover cloth, which she shed in her effort to escape.

Quick thinkingly, he had let her get away and had fumbled around the table to find out how McKeown had fared. He found him already sagging forward with his head amongst the dishes, found the garrotte and had it free of McKeown's neck in a matter of seconds. He then laid the man flat on the floor and raised his feet onto a chair.

McKeown, who was almost unconscious, drew breath back into his lungs with a great rasping sound and soon stirred under Lassiter's hands.

By the time the waiters had lit candles and oil lamps, McKeown had his eyes open.

The two girls got away, but from that evening on, the CIA man found it impossible to continue the kind of surveillance that was expected of him.

He therefore informed his Reports Officer that he considered the State Department's suspicions of Lassiter to be unfounded and that he was going to concentrate his main effort on one of his other projects—the penetration, through the use of a locally recruited agent, of the Communist-led Students Union at the local university.

A few months later, Lassiter died in circumstances which left McKeown wondering whether, after all, the clearance he had given Lassiter had been accepted.

"I travelled to Syria and remained there for two years. I had no other objective than that of seeking solitariness, overcoming selfishness, fighting passions, trying to clear my soul, to complete my character," Mamadou read.

And a little later he came to, "The Sufis are not men of words but of inner perceptions. I had learned all that could be learned from reading. The remainder could not be acquired by study or talk."

His acquaintance with Quarshie and the work he had done for him, Mamadou decided, sitting in his austere little room waiting for a call, had produced a turning point in his life, a catalysis.

What he was reading came from the work of Ghazali, the Spinner, and what this great Sufi leader had, in effect, said was that if there was an urgent undertaking in life which bears a relationship to one's future, what one does about it will matter very much. If no such undertaking is in sight, then inaction does not matter. He, Mamadou, had reached the age when he was going to have to make a decision between the two undertakings which tempted him. His activities under Quarshie's guidance had satisfied one of them. Sitting quietly in meditation in his room filled the other.

He knew now that, for the moment, the latter was the most important and gave him the most satisfaction. When his work with Quarshie was done he would become a true, full-time student of the Sufi masters until he felt that he, too, had "learned all that could be learned from reading." Then he would apply himself to the quest for the divine knowledge, which "is so deep that it is really known only to those who have it."

And in case he became too overawed by the task he had set himself, he recalled and determined to remember always the words of the Persian Sufi, Nizami: "Under the poet's tongue lies the key of the treasury."

Some of the expatriates living in Fort Etienne thought of old Annie Bestward as a bit crazy, or at least as an eccentric, though they conceded that she was quite harmless. She was known by the authorities to have a little money in a bank in America, so she neither begged nor borrowed, nor did she get into debt. In addition, she had, in the past, given of her time and energy freely to help the sick and the destitute of Transniger, and there were many men and women, amongst them the General, who were grateful to her.

She called the small cement-block building in which she lived on the edge of the town, The New Jerusalem, and she ran a Christian mission all on her own there which bore no resemblance to any other that was to be found trying to convert the unbaptised to accept Christianity.

When anyone asked her to which denomination she belonged she was apt to reply, "There are two hundred and sixty Christian sects in my country, and I could never be bothered to examine them all to find out what they were about. To join me in The New Jerusalem you need only to visit me there, hear The Word, and meditate in silence on what it means."

Now she was old, too old to work. In the past she had spent most of her day up on the slopes of the hill, well out of town, where the lunatics were housed in small concrete huts closed in by high barbed-wire entanglements, or perhaps with the lepers in their settlement, or maybe in a village where there had been an outbreak of cholera or an epidemic of dysentery.

At her house, the room she called The Sanctum was as austere as the interior of a Muslim mosque. There was a block of rough-hewn pink stone at one end of it which carried on it a cross made of two plain, unpolished pieces of wood from an odum tree imported from Akhana. Facing the cross, some twenty feet from it, was a locally made *prie-dieu* with a Bible open on it. The room was floored with red tiles, and there were mosquito screens on the windows. After dark, the room was lit by two candles, one on the altar and one beside the *prie-dieu.*

The rest was only whitewashed walls and dark roof beams with whitewashed mud between them.

On a notice outside the gate there was an inscription in English and French and, in Kufic script, in Arabic: "Meditation on the Holy Word. Every evening. All are welcome." And beside the message there was a door which every evening stood wide open so that passers-by could see the kneeling figures inside.

Old Annie had of late allowed herself a slight dispensation from the extreme austerity of her surroundings. She had made herself a small hassock.

Every evening she read aloud from the Bible on her *prie-dieu,* repeating every twenty minutes the passage she had selected for the day.

Over the years she had developed the habit of never looking around or away either from the Bible or from the Crucifix. She always said that her spirit told her when she had others with her to share her worship.

On the night of the Big M's attempted massacre, she had no guards because no one in authority had remembered her existence, so she was kneeling, as she had been kneeling every night at that time, for twenty-five years, and she was alone with "The Word."

A little earlier she had read aloud to the empty room one of her favourite passages from the Bible. It came from Isaiah.

In a voice which quavered with age she started her quotation with the words,

"To what purpose is the multitude of your sacrifices unto me? saith the Lord. I am full of burnt offerings of rams, and the fat of fed beasts: and I delight not in the blood of bullocks, or of lambs, or of he-goats . . ." And she ended with, "Wash you make you clean: put away the evil of your doings from before mine eyes; seek judgement, relieve the oppressed, judge the fatherless, plead for the widow."

The words sang in old Annie's heart, and she was in such a state of exaltation in her ancient soul when the noose of the garrotte tightened around her throat that she was hardly aware of it and died without a struggle. She was, perhaps, Arrani's most innocent victim.

After she had done her work, the assassin pinched out the flames on both candles, because she felt that it would be a waste to leave them lit, and then departed as quietly as she had arrived.

The young man was intent on his task. He was welding an elaborate piece of wrought-iron scrollwork into place in the already made-up frame of a window grille.

He was still attacking the job with enthusiasm, though most of the inhabitants of Fort Etienne were already asleep. The grille was a part of the first large order he had received, and the money he would earn from it meant that quite soon he would be able to buy a car instead of being almost the only European in Fort Etienne who had to ride to work on a bicycle.

He worked at night because, in the daytime, he taught the art of welding at the local trade school.

To protect his eyes from the brilliance of the oxyacetylene flame he had to wear dark glasses set in a thick rubber frame, fitted closely around his eyes, which reduced his peripheral vision to virtually nil.

He came from Sicily. His name was Salvatore Riccobana, and he had only been in Africa for four months.

The assassin who killed him stayed to watch him die, taking pride in the fact that she, a little black girl, could kill such a big, strong white man.

When he was dead, she took off his dark glasses and removed everything he had in his pockets. On second thought, she started to undress her victim with the idea of making a present of his clothes to her brother. If she had known the phrase, she might have called what she planned to take from him "the spoils of war."

She was acting against the orders she and all her sister assassins had been given by the Big M, and she paid for her disobedience with her life.

The torch Salvatore had been using was still burning when he dropped it and it fell, so that the flame was directed at a spare bottle of gas which stood alongside his workbench.

It took a little while for the metal casing of the gas bottle to heat to the point where it would cause the gas bottle to explode, just long enough, in fact, for the girl to remove Salvatore's shirt and start to unbuckle his belt.

The sound of the detonation woke a surprisingly large number of heavy sleepers in the neighbourhood and it collapsed the garage in which Salvatore had been working.

A few Europeans living in the country had been able to develop a "father of the house" relationship with some of the people of Transniger, though in most cases such connections had an association with business.

The most notable example of a white man who had established a "family" was a Greek named Papas. He was the local manager of CPAO, one of the French trading companies which had developed extensive holdings throughout West Africa during the colonial period.

One of the assets of the post that Papas held was that it enabled him to sell goods at wholesale prices to a company he had formed and operated himself in the name of an African trader.

No one except the most immediate members of this Transnigerian "family," of which he was the "father of the house," knew of his connection with it.

Nor did Papas, through this operation, shortchange CPAO. He worked close to a sixteen-hour day, every day, ten or twelve of them for his French employer, and the rest of the time on his own business. CPAO dealt in wholesale as well as retail business, so he was not engaged in any affairs which meant that he had to falsify the statements in his account books. At the same time, his principals were well-satisfied with the size of the profits—indeed they paid him a considerable bonus on them, and if they suspected him of using his position to his own advantage there was plenty of precedent for it.

Most of the time and often far into the night, Papas worked in his office over the main CPAO store on the Boulevard de la Liberté in the centre of the city.

Arrani's plan for his girl's attack on Papas involved her climbing over a wall into the CPAO compound and then, with a small iron bar, prising some boards off a basement window which had been smashed accidentally by workmen unloading a truck and nailed up to await the installation of a complete new window frame. The plan took into account the existence, both inside and outside the compound, of night watchmen. The one outside was to be distracted by the girl who had killed the Russian. And she was given a young cockerel in a box which was to be let loose as soon as she dropped down inside the wall. Then, while the inside night watchman tried to capture it to take home to his wife, she was to get on with her job. It was the most complicated of all Arrani's plans, and it almost worked.

Where it failed was in its last phase. This called for the girl to walk up the stairs to the floor on which Papas had his office and make her way into his secretary's office through which he would have to pass when he left. Since she could not walk into his office and kill him, because his desk faced the doorway, she was to lock the outer door and when he came out and was struggling with it, she was to attack him from behind.

What Arrani failed to anticipate was that Papas, who often had large sums of money out on his desk as he checked them before banking them, took two precautions against an attack by a thief.

The first was that a desk light was always left burning in the outer office, and it was focused on the ground-glass panel of door which connected that office to his own.

With her heart beating rather fast because of her exertions and rather pleased with herself because of her success so far, the girl was completely nonplussed by finding the light.

Aware that it would have to be put out, she stood in front of it with her back to Papas' door trying to locate the switch.

Papas' second precaution was that he always kept a loaded revolver in his desk. Seeing her shadow starkly outlined on the ground glass and without investigating any further, he fired a carefully aimed shot.

The girl, standing no more than twenty feet away, was hit in the head and died instantly.

When Papas opened the door he called the police and returned to his bookkeeping until they arrived to question him. It was the police officer who established that she was one of the Big M's killers, because she was carrying a garrotte in a small cloth bag concealed under the bodice of her dress and hung around her neck on a drawstring.

Arrani was not the only person capable of making miscalculations —Quarshie could do it too. He had, in fact, done it when he believed that by taping the conversation between the girls who were put in the communal cell for the Big M's employees he could pick up some useful evidence. The first two girls, who came together there, had only a very rudimentary knowledge of the one language they had in common.

Their exchange, when it was played back, sounded like this:

"It is not good."

"No, it is not good."

"The Master not be happy."

"It is so."

"You did not kill?"

"I did not."

"More have not killed?"

"I do not know."

"It is bad."

"It is bad."

Silence.

"I did not kill."

Silence.

"It is bad."

"It is bad."

The third silence continued for a very long time and was broken eventually by the sound of one of the girls singing a song very softly in her own language.

Since the tape machine, one of only a dozen or so in Fort Etienne, was not provided with any means of monitoring what was being recorded, the tape was allowed to run to the end and was then replaced with a new one to retain, as Quarshie said ruefully afterwards, the longest session of nonintelligence that anyone had ever taken the trouble to preserve.

Arrani found that waiting in the truck by himself was a trying experience. He was the commander who had to wait out of sight over the horizon while his subordinates gave battle. The issue depended on them and was out of his hands, though the plan of attack was his.

In this operation he, Arrani, was the tactical planner, the master killer. He had set up all the assassinations. Those who died did so because he had sentenced them.

Seen objectively, at this point in the operation, had the choices of victims been as truly random as they were supposed to be? He wondered.

The honest answer was, No.

Some of those who were to die had been selected for personal reasons. Others for the sake of convenience.

The *stagiare* at the French Embassy had, in fact, chosen himself by pushing in front of Arrani at the bank one day, trading on his colour and his friendship with the General, to get preferential treatment. Rykowski had refused a black man a blood transfusion, and the man had died. The pregnant wife of a Canadian had been chosen by the Big M because he had seen her one day in a store with her swollen belly, and he had decreed that whites should be discouraged from spawning on African soil.

Then there were others whom, one could say, almost offered themselves to the garrotte, like the old missionary woman and the young Italian, because they made it so easy for the girls to kill them.

At that point in his reconsideration of his work, he saw the Big M and Kali coming towards him across the lorry park.

When they were in the cab of the truck beside him, Kali told him that the girl who had been the first to report at the rendezvous was the one who had killed old Annie Bestward. The Master had embraced her and in a fit of enthusiasm had given her fifty American dollars. Then he had ordered her to get on the next lorry that would take her back to her village, where she was to keep her mouth shut and wait until he sent for her again.

After the girl had left, the Big M had said, Kali told Arrani, "Now is the time for us to get lost. As the body count grows, all hell is going to break loose here."

Leaving the city the young man drove a different route to the one he had followed on the way in. At the roadblock, to establish his validity as a local citizen, he had started off excitedly recounting what he said were market rumours of a big attack on the whites by the assassins. Then, before the corporal in charge of the police at the roadblock could respond in any way, he went right on to explain the Big M and Kali, now dressed to match the role, as Tuaregs who were returning to their camp in the Sahara. Still without a pause, he explained that he was going to give this brother and sister in Allah a lift part of the way because otherwise they would have a very long distance to travel on foot. The corporal gave up trying to stem the flood of words, glanced at the registration, insurance and road worthiness papers, which Arrani handed him, noted the number of the vehicle and waved them on. He had no orders to stop and search Tuaregs. With the Big M's stature, blue robes and ancient Dane gun, and Kali dressed in the same coloured cloth with a veil over her face that left only her eyes in view, the corporal had seen no reason to question their identity.

A few miles after the roadblock they turned off the road and took to open country. With the Big M navigating a compass course, they made a diagonal interception of the route they usually took to their rock-bound hideout. They came back into territory they could identify soon after dawn and then drove north at the best speed they could make with the two men driving in turns.

When they reached Alamut, late in the afternoon, they loaded the truck with several months' supply of dried and canned foods, water, fuel, and all their guns and ammunition. Then they headed deeper into Africa towards another rock pile with caves in it two hundred miles further on. It was somewhere in the wide rubble- and rock-strewn desolation of the Sahelian Sahara that the Big M, speaking hoarsely from a dust-filled throat and with sweat streaming from every pore, had said, "No fugitive in history ever had wider horizons into which to escape than we have. The area is over three thousand miles wide by fifteen hundred across, and, brother, if we can't get lost in that amount of real estate, then I guess even outer space would not be big enough for us."

Morgan Morgan, as his name indicated, was a Welshman. He had come from Merthyr Tydfil in the Rhondda Valleys, via Cardiff University, to teach biology at the University of Transniger.

He had two enthusiasms which bordered on fanaticism and was developing a third. Before everything else he was a socialist, but running a close second came the conviction that the only science which was truly relevant was biology. Now he was developing an equally strong predisposition to the idea that the way to equalize the rich and the poor in the Third World countries was to explain to as many young Africans as he could reach that, biologically, it was natural for all men to have certain needs, and that the only just society was one that was structured so that these needs could be met.

He had heard a lot about and had seen the consequences of the Great Depression in the valleys around his home, the running down, at that time, of the coal pits, the closing of the huge steel mill at Dowlais, and the development of a mass of men who had had to live for so long on welfare that they had rotted away and had become unemployable—men who would normally have possessed his bounding vitality. The memory of what, in his words, "My da told me, boyo, of the terrible emptiness of life around the pit head towns in the valleys . . ." became a spectre which haunted him.

Everywhere he looked around him now he saw empty lives, and the need to fill them gave him the sense of purpose, energy and dedication he needed to fight the heat, bureaucratic obstruction and passivity of his students. Another problem he had had to confront was the rigid notions so many of them had fixed in their minds by the, as Morgan Morgan saw it, antiquated, old Testamanic fury of the teachings of the Koran.

"That book does not talk about life, man . . . ," he had told one of his more fanatical Muslim students, ". . . it only talks about death and war, about killing and torturing your enemies for the sake of some purely fantastical reward in some sort of future life. Biology *is* life, and the study of it can bring you rewards that are greater than any prophet or god can promise you for the future." He was particularly concerned with the would-be students who had not had the means, or perhaps the ability, to be accepted into the university but were still interested in learning. "They have minds like sponges, man, and they draw up inspiration as fast as you can pour it out for them," he had once written home to a friend. For those who could not attend the university he held a private class in a mud hut provided by one of his wealthier converts.

Amongst those who came to the classes was a young girl whose attendance was irregular but who always brought papers which showed unusually creative approaches to the subjects they had been discussing. They had, in fact, been prepared by Arrani.

She was a pretty girl and she usually stayed behind after the others left while he read through her paper. It was a brief moment or two in his hard-working week that he looked forward to, because not only were the papers interesting but, he felt, somewhere in the contact he detected a hint of affection, something which set them apart, a black girl and a white man, two pigeons in a flock of crows.

On this particular evening she pretended to be annoyed when he tried to hold her hand and went and stood behind his chair looking over his shoulder while he read her paper, but she held the side of her face against his ear with a tenderness that made him want to move closer to her. Then he came upon a line in the text which he had trouble deciphering and moved his head towards the paper to see it better, and at that moment the cord bit tightly around his throat. Once it was locked in place, the girl put her hands over his eyes and with surprising strength held his head against her breasts. Somewhere in the strange emotions which filled her at the moment she, too, was conscious in some peculiar way that she loved him, and for a long time after he was dead she continued to hold his head against her breasts, bewildered by her unexpected sexual response in his last futile struggle.

Those countries which accepted aid from Israel found it to be the most effective and best suited to their needs, next to that from Mao's China or Formosa. In all three cases the money was not given to be used for prestige developments which advertised their donors loudly and with displays of flags; nor was the Israeli or Chinese money spent on glittering technological projects. Their aid was usually unashamedly utilitarian, relating to food production or the development of the country's own resources in such a way as to make it less dependent on imports.

Mordecai Avny was a Sabra. He stood a fraction over six feet tall, weighed two hundred pounds, all of it bone and muscle, had a thick head of black hair, and was twice as strong and energetic as any of the men on the farm where he worked raising cattle by crossbreeding Brahma bulls with other imported stocks. The object of his work was to increase both the meat and the milk yield of the animals in the experimental herd that he was building.

Like most Israelis and Chinese and unlike most other directors of aid projects, Mordecai worked with his African labourers in the field. This made him popular with those around him but most unpopular with many others, because commanding a workforce amongst elite Transnigerians was something which was done from the back of a horse or, when they could afford it, from the seat of a Landrover. They felt that he was betraying the natural privileges of the ruling classes.

Although he worked with the men, he did not fraternise with them very much. His hobby was photography and, apart from a youth whom he was training to be a photographer and who also went everywhere with him, he spent very little time with anyone outside his regular hours of work.

He let it be widely known that he had nothing in his house worth stealing. He made one exception to his Spartan way of life. Being virtually a professional photographer, he had a special room which served as a darkroom as well as a storeroom for his photographic equipment. The room was inside the house, built of concrete blocks, and had no window, only an air conditioner and a steel door with double locks on it. He had built the room himself and had made all the installations in it.

All this meant that, aside from the darkroom, the keys of which were chained to his belt, he could safely leave the outer doors of his house unlocked at any time.

So the girl who came to kill him had no trouble getting inside. He was working in the darkroom after a late dinner when she arrived, and she remained out of sight for several minutes behind a fold in the wall. Then, when he came out to go to his bedroom—to fetch something, she thought—she slipped across the intervening space into the darkroom. There she placed herself so that she would be behind the door when he opened it.

However, the door did not open for five days. Only a few moments after she had entered it, Mordecai remembered that he had not locked it and had returned to correct that error.

The next morning he drove south to spend a short holiday with Israeli friends. Before he left he told his cook and his steward to take five days off too, and then for once he locked every door in the house and turned off the water.

When he came back at the end of his holiday, he found the girl collapsed on the floor of the darkroom, unconscious. She had been overcome by lack of oxygen and by thirst and hunger. He revived her with artificial respiration, examined her thoroughly, found the garrotte, and sent one of his staff into town to fetch the police.

At the point where the General called his Chef de Cabinet into his office, four would-be assassins had been captured and only Morgan Morgan's death had been discovered.

The General was cautiously optimistic about their terrorist countermeasures.

Amongst the orders he had signed earlier had been one enforcing a complete news blackout on everything connected with the assassinations, and he asked his aide now how he felt this would affect Quarshie. Was he a man, he wanted to know, who would be upset if his work did not receive public recognition?

The Chef de Cabinet shook his head. "The man is not human," he replied. "I am sure he is not looking for any rewards."

"Not human, but perhaps exceptionally humane?" the General offered.

This time the Chef de Cabinet shrugged. "Whatever that means. He will get plenty of limelight whether he wants it or not. Perhaps he is, in fact, very subtle and knows that the best way to obtain the most recognition is to avoid seeking it."

The General smiled. "My dear Ibrahim, you are very consistent in the way you believe the worst of everybody."

The Chef de Cabinet returned the smile and made a little bow. "It is an attitude I have to take, Your Excellency, to counterbalance your determination to see the best in them."

"And, as you know, it is an attitude that is of great value to me. What will you do when I am dead? Will you try to take my place and become, as you say I am, determinedly optimistic?"

"I would be ill-advised if I did. I could never live up to the image you will leave behind. No," he continued reflectively, ". . . but I might do worse than try to get Quarshie to take your place. He is a tolerant, sentimental man whom I can respect, and then we would have the same strengths at the head of the government that we have now."

"Are we so alike, he and I? If we are, then you will have the opportunity to start the wheels turning in the direction you have just suggested quite soon." The General stood up and fetched himself a glass of water from an earthenware cooler. "I have just been talking on the telephone with my friend the French Ambassador in Akhana, and he asked for permission to join us, bringing Mrs. Quarshie with him. He said he is having trouble with her and that she has virtually accused him of aiding and abetting us to kidnap the good Doctor. I said they should come as soon as they can. Your rather austere manner with women, I have noticed, makes you attractive to them. So perhaps you will exercise a little of your aristocratic charm on her to get into her good graces, because, whatever happens, she must not be allowed to distract him from his work."

The Chef de Cabinet nodded, leaving unexpressed his feeling that, from what he had heard about Mrs. Quarshie, she would be more likely to use successfully her charm on him. Whichever way it went, he thought, it might prove to be an interesting encounter.

A similar thought crossed the General's mind at the same moment, but he, too, left it unspoken.

The young woman in the well-starched white frock was carrying a large bundle tied up in a sheet of plastic on her head. As she passed under the street lamp her shadow went from a grotesque shape like an outsized lollipop on a stick behind her to the same shape ahead of her before switching over and dropping behind her again.

Then, as she was about to enter a gateway into a compound, two soldiers came out of the darkness of the bushes nearby and stopped her. They were men who came from a tribe which was centred in an area several hundred miles away from Fort Etienne. Instead of being cowed by their guns, the girl immediately turned on them and rudely demanded what they thought they, "bush bush men from a bush bush" area, were doing interfering with the freedom of passage of a lady of Fort Etienne who was about her lawful business, delivering laundry.

The soldiers said that if she wanted to enter the compound they would have to search her.

She responded with a torrent of words which could be summed up in a single sentence—that she would see them in the hottest part of Muslim hell before she allowed them to put a dirty pagan finger on her. And she called loudly and by name for the house steward to come and rescue her from the attentions of two evil-smelling soldiers who were determined to molest her.

The steward, of the same tribe as the girl and also a Muslim, appeared immediately and spoke to the two soldiers in a tone of superiority that matched the one the girl had used. If the men insisted on their intention to assault the girl, he said, which as everyone knew was the kind of behaviour to be expected from sex-starved soldiers from the far bush, then he would have to call the master and have him report the men's behaviour to their officer.

It was a deadlock.

The soldiers kept their bayonets pointed at the girl, and when she took a step forward the bayonets came forward as well.

It was tribal warfare, with great reluctance on both sides to modify their aggressive attitudes and thus to lose face.

The steward was the eldest of the small gathering, and it was traditionally his duty to bring some kind of order.

In a more reasonable tone of voice he said, "The master knows this girl. I will go and ask him if she may be allowed in without the indignity of being searched." He did not wait for agreement from the soldiers but turned his back on them and walked away.

When he came back he had not seen the white man who occupied the bungalow, but pretended that he had.

"The man says she may come. You are not to touch her." He spoke quietly and without arrogance.

"Then he is responsible for what happens," said one of the soldiers, "and you, too, who brought the message and therefore could have falsified it. The men of Fort Etienne are known all over Transniger to be liars."

The two men lowered their guns and returned to their post outside the gate, and the steward decided, reluctantly, to ignore the parting insult.

As he and the girl walked together towards his quarters at the back of the house he told her, "Today we must examine our accounts, thou and I. There is money owing for the amount of laundry I obtain for you, for the dash the man gives you, and now for arranging that little matter with the soldiers. The man asked me only yesterday whether I thought he gave you enough and I told him it should be more, so today you will receive more, and half of it is for me."

He expected the girl to remonstrate but she did not.

The master of the house was a Belgian employed by the United Nations on a special intermediate technology project. He was a retired businessman from a city he called Anvers. He was also a lonely and dissatisfied man. He missed both his wife and his job, and his heart was not in his work in Fort Etienne but in the memories of the petite, generous woman who had shared his bed, his home, his ambitions, pleasures and disappointments for over thirty years. He also missed the satisfaction of being called *le patron* by his tugmasters, their crews and the lightermen.

In Fort Etienne he was trying to set up a limited freight transport system on the river, but the frustrations—some of them caused by ignorance, others by human failure, and others by the heat shifting sand banks in the river—were almost too great to be borne by a man of his age.

Even worse than these interferences with his happiness were the long evenings he spent alone in his bungalow. It was then that the feelings of futility really crowded in on him, nudging him deeper and deeper into melancholy. In an effort to hold off the threat to his sanity, he found his hand reaching out more and more often towards the neck of the brandy bottle, or towards any distraction which took his mind clear of the Scylla of the bittersweet nostalgia and the Charybdis of his present pointless existence. Actually, what was happening, he realised, was that the one was destroying any worthwhile satisfaction he could get from the other.

So, one of his most looked-forward-to distractions was the occasional visit he received from a young woman who brought clean linen from a washerwoman who not only kept his personal things immaculate but also starched his bed linen in a way that he had not known since his boyhood on the family estate near Villers le Gambon.

Clean sheets on his bed every night was an extravagance which he allowed, partly because he enjoyed the cool slipperiness of the sheets on his skin as he got into bed at night, and partly because he enjoyed the pert young woman who came in, swinging her hips, to ask for her money after she had made her delivery. She spoke French fluently with an incongruously strong Marseillaise accent which amused him. All the time, too, she played a provocative little game with him, talking at one moment as if she was his daughter, and the next like a cheerful little strumpet bent on seducing him. He knew that it was for his benefit that she wore preposterously short skirts, that she sat on low stools with her knees slightly apart, or bent over with her back towards him to pick up something which she had dropped quite deliberately.

The cost to him for this entertainment, for he never went beyond the mild voyeurism that she encouraged by her behaviour, was so little that he did not even count it. The favours she bestowed on him were offered for the small change she made out of him in dashes.

This evening she came into the livingroom where he was relaxing in a long chair, offered him very correct salutations, asked after her "father's" health, dropped him the little bobbing curtsey she had learned at the convent where she had been trained by nuns from Provence, and enquired politely whether he had done anything exciting since she had seen him the last time.

Then she plumped herself down on the floor in front of him, sitting with her shoulders back against the arm of a chair, with her knees up and her feet apart, and launched into a rapid and exaggerated tale of the infamous treatment she had received not only from the soldiers outside the gate but from soldiers everywhere. She made all their actions lascivious, and presently she found she had to stand up to mime the way she had to twist her hips out of the way of men with predatory fingers. When she considered that she had given enough of that performance she switched to the role of a little girl pretending to be excited about finding items in the room which filled her with curiosity. She found a small-scale model of a tugboat cast in brass, a transparent paperweight with edelweiss in it, three tiny Japanese parasols which could be opened and closed, and the outer casing of a Brazil nut with the shell polished and carved so that it was possible to see the precise packing of the nuts inside it. And he had to tell her the exact story, as he had told her many times before, of each item.

At a certain point in all this ritual he became aware that their relationship was not in the same balance that it had always been in the past. Her role-playing was more than usually artificial, and she was plainly nervous. Also, she seemed to be trying to get behind him all the while, and this made him uneasy. Once, when he turned suddenly, it appeared as if she hid something behind her back.

Finally he turned his chair slightly so that he could watch what was taking place behind him in the reflection in the glass covering a painting.

Thus he surprised her, the third time he became suspicious of the way she was approaching the back of his chair, by getting quickly to his feet and turning so fast that she did not have time to conceal the garrotte she was holding in her hands.

Though he was over sixty-five he was a sinewy little man, and he seized her wrists in a grasp which was surprisingly powerful, and for the second time that evening the girl found herself deadlocked.

There followed a moment of immobility and silence while they each one tried to decide what to do next.

For his part, it was only when he realized that she might have murdered others, or continue to murder others, that he decided to call the soldiers. If he could have been sure that he was designed to be her only victim, he might simply have taken the toggled cord away from her and given her a chance to escape.

So far as the girl was concerned, she had never considered what she would do if she came close to being caught, because she never thought such a thing would happen. She was strong as well as plump, and desperation made her stronger. By turning her wrists downward against his thumbs she broke his grip and darted away towards the door more quickly than he could follow her. Then she ran blindly and foolishly out of the house and down the driveway towards the gate in a completely thoughtless panic.

In a rather half-hearted way the Belgian stepped out onto the verandah and shouted after her, "*Arrêtez cette fille, là. Arrêtez la.*" An order the soldiers obeyed with enthusiasm. They caught her and brought her to the ground so hard that she had all the wind knocked out of her.

She had dropped the garrotte as she ran out of the livingroom, and the Belgian picked it up and took it to the men at the gate, one of whom was sitting on his captive's face. Taking a handful of hair, he twisted her savagely over onto her stomach and resumed his position, this time on the back of her head, forcing her nose and mouth into the dust.

When they had secured her wrists with the garrotte they hauled her to her feet, and the senior of the two soldiers took his rifle and went to fetch the steward at gunpoint.

When he returned with his prisoner he told the Belgian in broken *petit nègre*, "Dissa man, bad man. Humbug too much. Work wid dis bad woman. I go take him for polis station alonga her." And to forestall any protest by the steward, he struck him hard on the back of the head with the brass heel of his rifle.

It was tribal warfare again, and the fortunes of war had swung over to put the other side in the strongest position.

The man and the girl were then prodded and thumped down the road in the direction of the centre of the town, suffering not only a number of painful blows on their backs and rumps but also a lot of coarse badinage along with them.

After he had watched them out of sight the Belgian returned disconsolately to his livingroom, where he drank the better part of a bottle of brandy, went to bed and cried himself to sleep out of loneliness, too much alcohol and sorrow for himself, the girl and the rest of the world.

Amélie Afif had been designed for spinsterhood since the day she left her mother's womb. She was ugly, as dry as straw, yet willfully and uncommonly strong and obstinate. Only her garden, the thing she cherished most in her life, rebelled against her. She worked furiously at it whenever she had the time, but little that she planted in it grew, though she watered the beds so heavily that her bill for water was three times as high as anyone else's in the town. Water was a very expensive commodity in Fort Etienne.

Her mother had been a Frenchwoman. She had lived in Ismailia and had married an Egyptian.

Amélie worked for the International Commission for Birth Control and Population Restraint, and she believed fanatically that motherhood was treated as a personal indulgence by most women and could, on occasions, even be regarded as a cardinal sin. Total abstinence from sex was her answer to the problem of "population restraint," even though in this opinion she was not really in accord with the guidelines set out in the Commission's charter.

When anyone remonstrated with her she always replied that she had lived in celibacy all her life without suffering any deleterious effects, so why should not others? "Ants," she used to say, "people are like ants swarming all over the place. A plague of ants."

Though her garden failed to respond to her fanatical attentions, she worked at it fiercely, getting up before dawn every day to start her labours.

For several months now she had employed a stranger to help her. She was a girl who could purchase manure for her which she brought in panier loads on the back of a donkey. The girl would stay and help Amélie to distribute the stuff around the garden.

It was that task upon which they were employed in the early dawn of the day following the start of the Big M's major offensive.

The girl carried the manure in a basket on her head and dumped it in small piles on the flowerbeds. Amélie then spread it over the earth.

It was while she was bending forward engaged upon this task that the girl came from behind her and killed her. From the position she was in, it was inevitable that she should fall forward into a patch of newly spread cattle dung and, after one or two convulsive archings of her back, die there.

The girl finished distributing the manure and then walked in a leisurely way down to the river, where she washed the reek of ordure out of her clothes and her hair.

As other girls were brought into the cell, the conversation became much freer and the microphone and tape recorder picked up a lot of chatter, some of it excited, some of it fearful, and some of it disappointed.

To Quarshie, reading in the early hours of the morning a transcript of the most important parts of the tape, it became clear that the organisation he was dealing with was led, as he supposed already, by two Afro-Americans and a Transnigerian.

They had a base roughly thirty-six hours' drive to the northwest of Fort Etienne.

The girls had been chosen for their work more or less at random and had then been indoctrinated with a blind sense of hatred for the whites.

The man they called the Master was worshipped and feared in much the same way as "true believers" worshipped and feared Allah. The roles played by the other two were less distinct. Kali, the woman, was also feared. The role of Arrani, the Transnigerian, was less well-defined beyond the fact that he served as the Master's linguist.

They had guns and a truck.

Those girls who failed in their task of killing, or were insubordinate, were murdered with a considerable amount of obscene ceremonial.

The Master's word was absolute.

One comment suggested that he had plans to kill millions of whites.

One of them had spoken of a sackful of American money and of walking into a cave and finding Arrani sitting beside the sack counting the money.

The report concluded with a statement that the police had seen nothing of the ringleaders in town that day.

Much of the recording, Quarshie thought, could be used as evidence at a trial, but there was little which offered any sort of leverage for a man who wished to turn the whole structure over and destroy it.

Fatou Attasy was the largest of the Big M's girls. She was also the eldest and the most intelligent. Curiously, however, it was Arrani who attracted her more than the Master, and he was the reason she stayed with the group. She saw through the Big M, recognising, without being able to articulate the thought, that he was a charlatan. At the same time she could see that there was sincerity in Arrani's beliefs.

For her own safety, however, and in order to stay with the group and therefore with Arrani, she submitted to the Master in everything that he asked of her. The largest part of his demands were sexual, which surprised her, and she wondered whether, perhaps, he knew that when he took her he never did so completely, that she always held back. And she wondered whether his persistence was fired by the fact that he treated it as a challenge, even a contest, in which his goal was to break into the ultimate corner of her being. Or, perhaps, as Kali told her one day, she just happened to be the only Big M-sized woman in the family.

Her assignment during the assault on the whites in Fort Etienne was to kill the white pregnant woman whom the Master had seen.

Fatou had not thought of her assignment very seriously until the moment when she was actually faced with it.

Her plan of action, or rather the plan Arrani had devised for her, was that she was to break into the house in the early hours of the morning and kill the woman in her bed as she slept. For this she was to use her bare hands, if she could not get the garrotte into place.

Arrani had learned, from the servants who worked in the house, that during her pregnancy the woman had elected to sleep in a room by herself.

Both the woman and her husband were French-Canadians, and he was the director of the Canadian Overseas Aid programme in Trans-niger.

Breaking into the house was a comparatively simple matter, because all the rooms gave onto a wide verandah that was screened with mosquito netting which could be cut quite easily.

When she got to the house Fatou found that it was also a simple matter to avoid the military guards, because one of the neighbouring bungalows bordered a piece of wasteland and all she had to do was to get through a hole in the acacia hedge and then find her way through similar holes in the hedges between the wasteland and the garden of the bungalow.

Nor had the night watchman been any obstacle. He was an old man and had been drowsing in his chair when she had come on him from behind and struck him on the head with a heavy stick with a piece of cloth wound around it. Then she had gagged him and tied him up very securely. Arrani had been insistent that she should not kill him, because he was a very devout Muslim.

In the end she had found it unnecessary to cut the wire screen, because someone had forgotten to lock the door into the outside and separate kitchen.

The two bedrooms in the bungalow were separated by the living-room. In the bedroom at the eastern end the husband was sleeping, with a rasping sound coming from his throat.

Fatou, barefooted, walked silently to the other end of the verandah where jalousied doors filled the central half of each of three doorways. Her plan had been to creep under the half doors and crawl to the side of the bed out of sight of its occupant, and she had just started to bend forward when she heard someone whispering quite audibly.

The words she heard were in French, a language she knew almost as well as her own, having passed with good marks through a French secondary school.

"You are my little cabbage, you understand?" was what she heard. "My darling. All that I have ever wanted."

At first Fatou thought that perhaps the woman had taken another man to bed with her, or perhaps there was a visitor sleeping in the room she had thought was occupied by the husband and that he had returned to her side for the night.

The whispered words were followed by a silence.

Fatou strained her ears to hear any other sounds, and before long the whispering started again.

"*Tu est mon bien aimé, tu compris? Mon mignon petit fils.*" Another pause. "Now that I have you, the world is a new and more wonderful place. Can you hear me? Or shall I have to wait until you leave me and become a being on your own? Is it enough that I just think the things I am telling you for you to understand? Anyway, it won't be very long now before I can hold you in my arms and talk to you, instead of just lying here with you inside me. In less than a week we shall be on a plane on our way back to Trois Rivières"—it sounded almost as if the woman laughed—"and then, quite quickly, we shall know whether I have been right to call you *mon favouri* instead of *ma favourite.* You won't hold it against me if I have been making a mistake, will you? Whether you are a little boy or a little girl makes no difference. I shall love you always. When you—no, I don't mean you—I mean when one says that to a man, it is not possible to be certain that it is quite true. But you, *ma poupée,* when you are small and take my milk I shall love you, and when you are bigger and take my hand I shall love you. And when you have brothers and sisters I shall have them for you to be your companions, and I shall have so much love that it will not be divided but a new quantity will come into being with each child, so you will never need to be jealous or to feel that anything is being taken away from you."

Fatou shivered.

The whispering continued but she did not listen.

Instead she listened to a voice inside her. It told her to go away, to leave the bungalow and the Big M, to leave killing to men and to seek what the whispering woman had found.

Men could not bring life into the world. They could only destroy it. But with the help of a man, if she were lucky, she could have a child to talk to the way the white woman was talking to her child, and that had to be the most important thing in the world.

As quietly as she had come, she left.

She looked at the night watchman on her way past him and saw that his eyes were open. What she had just discovered was something she had to share with somebody. So she patted his shoulder and told him, "Papa, I must tell you something. Listen . . ." And she told him of all that had happened since she first joined with the assassins and of the experience she had just had, and he, still gagged and bound, had to listen. At the end she said, "I am sorry I had to strike you, Papa. Ask Allah to forgive me for that. And tell the cook to lock his door after he leaves the house. Or perhaps you, Papa, were less than a good night watchman because you did not look to see whether the door was locked. Anyway, be patient, they will let you go very soon, when they find you. I am going now. Go with Allah, Papa." Then she raised his head and rolled up a spare cloth he had with him and put his head back on it and took her way back through the holes in the hedges and into the town.

As she passed down the Avenue du Grand Reveil, the African sparrows were starting to twitter sleepily in the trees and she had a feeling that she had been specially guided to walk down that particular street at that particular time of day to mark indelibly on her mind the meaning of the experience she had just passed through.

Mamadou was obviously elated when he came in to see Quarshie, who had slept for a couple of hours around dawn and was now eating his *petit déjeuner* in the restaurant of the Hotel Buffet de la Gare, which served both the travellers from the infrequent trains and the residents staying at the hotel.

At the moment the room seethed with people, a pushing, scrambling mass of them, because this was the time of day when the train left for the coast, the daily express grandly called "La Flèche du Kaya-Maghan." Kaya-Maghan was the title given to the rulers of ancient Ghana around the year 1,000 A.D. It meant "Lord of the Gold," and it referred to Ghana's great wealth.

The dominant mood amongst the people waiting for the eight-thirty departure of the train was anxiety: the swarming crowd vibrated with it.

Quarshie sat alone at a small table in a corner near the counter guarded by an old waiter in a white uniform who angrily and abusively kept men, women and children at a distance of at least six feet from the "big" man's table. He would also have held Mamadou at bay if Quarshie had not called to the old man to let his assistant through.

Mamadou's elation was so great that, after only the briefest greeting, Quarshie smiled at him and said, "Before you explode, tell me what's on your mind."

"Much has happened, sir, in the past few hours. At half past five a policeman searching people in a lorry found a girl carrying a large sum of money in American dollars. He detained her and the corporal in charge of the roadblock sent for me. I took her back under escort to the Central Police Station and, while I watched through a spy-hole, they put her in the cell with the other girls. They all greeted her at once, so she is obviously one of them, though she had denied it earlier. Via the microphone we also heard her tell the others that she had killed an old white woman. There are few old white women here, so the police are now checking on all those of whom they have knowledge."

"So we have another dead white?"

"Yes, sir and . . ." Mamadou checked his enthusiasm. "Yes, sir," he said in a quieter tone, "it is sad . . . but perhaps she did not die without purpose, as all the others did."

Quarshie took a bite of his *croissant* and moistened his mouthful with a sip of coffee. Then he nodded his head and said,

"I see. So what did you find out from the money?"

Mamadou looked surprised, was about to ask how Quarshie knew that the money would be important, thought better of wasting time with the question, and replied, "Rather a lot, sir. You may remember that one girl spoke of a sackful of money. The girl we captured was carrying dollar notes and they had consecutive numbers. I got my cousin from the Banque National out of his bed and we went and looked at the files in his office; he is the *vice-président*. The numbers on the bank notes showed that the money had been part of a ransom which was paid to some hijackers who held up a plane at Roberts Field in Liberia three years ago. Of course all the banks were alerted to look out for the money. After that, I had only to go to my uncle, get his keys for the newspaper office, and look in the back numbers of the paper. The circular with the list of bank notes on it was dated. Looking back from that day, I found a full account of the hijack with eyewitness descriptions of the hijackers. Two men and one woman, sir. One man was big, one was rather small. The woman, it was said, was heavily built. So . . . sir, we have them."

"We do? Where? Where are they?"

"No, sir. I don't mean that. I mean we have descriptions of them, and we know for certain who we are looking for."

Quarshie said kindly, "Yes. That was an excellent piece of detective work. You did very well. It is useful to know who you are looking for." And then in an equally gentle tone of voice he added, "Now all we have to do is to find them."

"Yes, sir." Mamadou still spoke with enthusiasm. Then he understood Quarshie's quiet irony and added in a different tone of voice, "I see what you mean, sir."

"I thought you would. You are quick to understand me. Now here is the next thing you have to do. Make enquiries everywhere you can about possible places where these people may have been camping. I don't think it would have been in or near a village, because that would make them the focus of too much attention. Nor do I think they would live in tents, not for as long as those women said that they had been in training. One of them said something about rocks and caves. So find a map and describe a couple of arcs on it with Fort Etienne as their centre. The first will represent the least distance they might have travelled with a lorry in thirty-six hours, say at a speed of ten miles an hour. That would be based on the possibility that they were going across rough country. Make the second arc to represent the distance they would cover at forty miles an hour. That would be how fast they might travel if they kept to good roads or reasonably good tracks. I don't think the place will be close to a road, because it would make it too easy for them to be discovered. Smoke from a fire, tracks in the sand leading from the road, indications like that would arouse too much curiosity. So I have a feeling that the area around the hideout will be more or less trackless. Then mark on the map all the possible places between the two arcs where there are cliffs or rocky outcrops in which there could be caves."

Quarshie put his big thick hand over the younger man's slender one as it rested on the table and concluded, "I think we are coming close to the end of this business. In another day or two we should be there. Your help has been very significant. Not the least part of it has been the gift I have received of your friendship. That, combined with the intelligence with which you do your work, has helped me immensely. Thank you."

And Quarshie wondered what a white man would say if he knew that his words made Mamadou blush.

Not long afterwards, when Quarshie had returned to his room and was preparing to leave again to go to the police station, Michel came to him.

Quarshie greeted him by saying, "When the owl is about in the daylight, it is an evil omen that no man should ignore. What brings you so early from your bed, friend?"

Michel was wearing dark glasses with huge circular lenses. Set against his white face and with his red hair clipped flat on the top of his head, he really did resemble an owl.

The young man shrugged and shook his head. "I am troubled, sir," he replied, "I could wish that what I saw was only that which was within the range of my eyes."

Quarshie put his arm around Michel's shoulders and walked with him to the rail of the verandah.

Below them the geometrically exact steel tendrils of the rail tracks stretched away into the distance towards a girder bridge over the Niger. To the left of the railway a large area of the landscape had been planted with ground nuts, and the small, dense foliage above the rows had turned to a rusty brown in the dry, scorching heat. A woman walked along beside the tracks carrying a pile of empty baskets on her head which more than doubled her height, and beyond her several large black carrion crows darted in and out nimbly between some vultures which were tearing at a pile of offal they had discovered in a heap of garbage.

After a few moments of silence Quarshie asked, "What did you see, my friend?"

"Sir, I am confused. It is like trying to remember a dream, or better, a nightmare. I cannot be certain of the . . . of the thing I saw. I know only that it made my heart grow weak inside me and filled my head with fearful darkness."

Quarshie said nothing but increased the strength of his grasp of the albino's shoulders.

"We were there, sir. You and Mamadou and I, and there was noise and dust . . . and death. One of those who died was very close to me and . . ." He shook his head. "I can't say it, sir. Must I?"

"Only *you* know the answer to that question, Michel."

The albino closed his eyes and Quarshie thought he had stopped breathing. Then, as if he were under the control of a ventriloquist, Michel said, "One of those who died was a very big man."

The three M's reached their destination as the heat of the morning was beginning to lean heavily on them. It had not been an easy journey. Their average speed had been very slow. They had stuck in a sand drift and had had to put strips of expanded metal, which they carried for the purpose, under the wheels before they could get the truck moving again.

Arrani, near the point of exhaustion, drove the vehicle into a cleft of the jebel, which was like a miniature fjord amongst the towering complex of rock pinnacles, with sand where there would have been sea had the fjord been a fact rather than a useful simile.

Then they ate and drank and lay down to sleep. They were overtired, their minds were overfull, and they had to spill some of their too abundant contents before any one of them could settle into the right pattern for sleep.

Kali unwound by thinking that she had "her" two men back again for the first time in months. The Bull and the Bantam were the words she used to describe them to herself. She had given up a long time ago trying to decide which of them she preferred. Both of them could and did satisfy her.

Both were hungry and decisive in their lovemaking, and perhaps, just perhaps, Arrani's vibrant, terrier-like intensity was the most amusing and satisfying. The fact that he had no desire to appeal to her maternal side pleased her at one moment, and in a niggling way distressed her at the next. The maternal drive was strong in her, as it is in most black women. Kali was a little distressed that her power over Arrani was so limited.

The Bull, on the other hand, was Man and Mate with a big M in both, and he had shown that he had needed her for other reasons, childlike ones. Alone, he wanted her to hold his hand and to tell him how clever he was. And now, she thought gratefully, I shall have weeks and perhaps months, to make these comparisons. Months when life would be raw, simple, and often made tedious by the heat and the sand, but made splendid, too, by looking up at the stars over one or the other of the shoulders of her companions.

The Big M thought of his arsenal. The guns in it had been acquired slowly and with care. His problem was one of choice, like Kali's. He found it difficult to decide which weapon was his favourite, the French MAT49 submachine gun, the AK47 automatic rifle made by the Russians, or the good old M15. In the end it usually came down to the American gun, because it had become such a willing friend in Vietnam. Of course, the MAT49 had its good points, too . . . and there were those who held that the AK47 was the best automatic rifle in the world. Well, they all had their uses, and first thing, when he had had a little sleep, he would check them out and oil them, maybe fire a few rounds from each of them, set up a target and show the others what a dead shot he was, no matter which gun he used.

Arrani's preoccupation was with his plans for a new anti-white terrorist group. First they would clear the countries of the Sahel of expatriates. They could look for support from Libya, Algeria and probably Iraq. It would be a real jihad against the whites, and to those who would argue that Africa needed help from Westerners, he would quote the words of the Koran, ". . . the alms which the infidels bestow in the present life are like a freezing wind, which falleth upon and destroyeth the cornfields of a people who have been to themselves unjust." Of course they would have to maintain diplomatic relations with the Western powers, but he would placard their embassies with billboards which read, "O ye who have believed! form no intimacies among others than yourselves. They will not fail to corrupt you. They will long for your ruin. Hatred hath shewn itself out of their mouths, but more grievous is what their breasts conceal . . . and when they meet you they say, 'We believe,' but when they are apart, they bite their finger ends at you out of wrath." And the Koran ordered that the believers say to the infidels, "Die in your wrath! God verily knows the very recesses of your breasts."

Yes, Arrani thought, with the Koran to advise him and inspire him, no man could fail to serve God as He demanded that men serve Him.

ELEVEN

. . . death . . . is . . . the price we have to pay for living . . .

Quarshie wrote in his diary: *I have just phoned the General's Chef de Cabinet and told him that we need the helicopter this afternoon. Mamadou has done his work well. I have a map with all the possible sites for the assassins' camp marked on it.*

The trip is to be merely a reconnaissance. If we find the right location we shall try to get some men out there to raid the place and to chase or capture any of the gang—they regard themselves as a "family"—who may stay to fight or try to run away.

At present the army and the police are carrying out a house-to-house search here, as well as checking all the traffic into and out of the city to try to pick up as many of the girls and their leaders as they can. We are assuming that quite a number of them are still here.

On a separate piece of paper Quarshie added an additional note.

Prudence, he told his wife, *if you read this note it will mean that I am dead.*

You may ask why I am continuing with this business if it looks as if I may be killed. I think Michel is afraid that he has foreseen my end. I am not really convinced. Nonetheless, I am leaving this au revoir *for you . . . just in case.*

You have known for a long time my view about death, that it is simply the price we have to pay for living, one that can be collected at any moment . . . suddenly and without warning.

Take that child who was killed by the assassins. At the most, she probably knew only a few seconds of anxiety and confusion, which can have lasted no longer than the transcendent moment of pleasure felt by her parents when they conceived her. So they paid for their earlier pleasure with the pain of her loss. Though it had to be more than that. And their hatred for those who caused their suffering will grow to include all men with black skins.

That fact underlies the business of the terrorist.

He is not expecting dividends from individual deaths but from creating mass horror and hysteria. Though, often, destruction for the terrorist is an end in itself, because he thinks that by destroying people who hold ideas with which he does not agree, he destroys the ideas themselves.

And I must stop them because the terror they create turns into a plague which excites men to kill indiscriminately without pausing to consider what they are doing. Nor do terrorists achieve anything of lasting value, because no one ever forgives a man who has terrified him into accepting something he does not believe in or does not want.

No, they create nothing but hatred, and any hatred of one man for another is barren or may give birth to monsters. You can hate an idea and work to change it, but to hate the man who has the idea is illogical and unproductive.

So why destroy the terrorists instead of trying to convert them?

Because they resist capture and reasoned argument with the same fanaticism with which they embrace violence.

Of course, we are not without blame in this picture, because terrorists often come into being for the reason that we condone injustices and may even help to originate them. So when we defeat the terrorist—and he must be defeated—we must right the wrongs which brought him into being.

There, I have intellectualised the thing—if that is not too big a word—and I can say to you what I cannot say to anyone else, that I know what I am talking about because I am a violent man myself. Therefore I know that violence is uncreative not just in theory but in fact. So, like the terrorist, it must be controlled by tolerance and reason. When it comes alive in me I feel that I can wipe out an evil force by wiping out a man. Only when I know that I am master of that blind impulse shall I be proud to be a man.

Prudence, my thought in writing these words was to tell you how grateful I am for what you have put into our life together, therefore what you have put into me. How formal that sounds.

I, too, have tried to put something into the life we have shared. Of course it was not the equal of what you put in, nor was it good enough, but it was there. So put that very small number into the credit column. My failures, if I know you, will not appear on the debit side. That will be because you are so generous, remembering only what is good.

Prudence, when you gave yourself to me, as you have in so many ways, you gave meaning to my life. It was never a case of you and I, but of the Quarshies, a unison, a harmony, one love.

If the worst happens, say au revoir *to Arimi. Tell him I expect him to fill my place beside you and to be a better man than I am.*

One has always to end a farewell abruptly, leaving ninety-nine per cent of it unsaid.

So, I must go—

allowing the rest of the page to remain blank—

knowing that you will fill it in with the words I have left unsaid but want you to say for me—

my Prudence

Quarshie left the note unsigned.

TWELVE

Don't want to sail in there and fly right down the barrel of a gun, do we?

Both Mamadou and Michel were feeling sick, and Quarshie was not too sure of the way his stomach was going to behave. Only the pilot of the helicopter seemed to be reasonably comfortable. They were no more than seven or eight hundred feet above the ground, flying at that height to be able to watch the patches of sand for wheel tracks. At that altitude the waves of heat, reflected upwards from rock and sand which created thermals, made the helicopter ride like a small ship in the aftermath of an Atlantic storm.

Here and there, in apparent wasteland beneath them, there were small settlements, a grouping of four or five round, small huts made of pale mud, thatched with elephant grass, and connected in a circle by thick camel-thorn hedges which enclosed a central area where a few goats could be kept at night to prevent them from straying.

Once the area had known lions, but now the parched, shadeless terrain offered little to satisfy their need for meat and no cover that they could use to stalk the few gazelle which still remained. So the lions had died out in the deprived Sahel Savannah where the goats the humans protected, the encroaching desert and bush fires, had stripped the land bare of greenery except for a few small thorny trees and acacia bushes that stood like ghosts of the vegetation which had once made the area green and fertile.

In rare patches where, during the short rainy season around the turn of the year, low-level land became flooded, there was intense cultivation of guinea corn, millet and yams. Also in a few isolated spots, where there was ground water, there were occasional clusters of date palms. The tiny spatterings of huts were often located close to these areas, but both human habitations and all vegetation gradually died out as the pilot took his machine a little west of north towards the sub-Saharan steppes.

The wheel tracks, which they saw only on rare occasions in drifts of sand, always kept well away from areas where men stubbornly continued to farm the parched earth.

Michel and Mamadou finally gave up and were sick into the paper bags the pilot had given them.

Quarshie, who was sitting next to the pilot, lost his queasiness in his interest in the land beneath him, in his map reading, and in his constant lookout for wheel tracks.

There had been some trouble in the beginning about including Michel in the crew instead of an armed policeman, but when Quarshie had insisted that he had the status of a secret weapon, and Mamadou, who was the only other person working on the project who knew of Michel's special gift, had supported him, the Chef de Cabinet had shrugged and given in. Though he had exacted a promise that Michel's role would be explained to him as soon as Quarshie had proven the young man's capabilities.

The moment they met, Quarshie felt at home with the pilot. Not only was he a fellow Akhanaian, but he had the typical joviality of his people, which was a characteristic that Quarshie found much less prevalent amongst the leaner Muslims, who had had to struggle for so many generations to persuade the arid land to satisfy their most basic needs.

The pilot's name was Captain Sogo, and he too had been delighted to see a fellow countryman. He had been trained to fly helicopters in England and had adopted, as had many other Africans who had been trained by the military in that country, what Quarshie spoke of to his wife as the "old boy syndrome." It was an accent and a vocabulary which often sounded like a parody of the British graduates of Sandhurst and Old Sarum, where the Africans had received their military instruction.

As if on cue, soon after they were airborne, Sogo came up on the intercom and said, "Put me in the picture a bit, will you, old boy? Like to have some sort of idea what we are up against, you know."

So Quarshie told him as much as he needed to feel that he was "in the picture."

"Any chance that things might get dicey, would you say?"

"It is always a possibility, I suppose."

"Not likely to have to put the old crate down and make an arrest, or anything like that?"

Quarshie said soberly, "They've got guns."

"Have they, eh? Well I've got a little pop gun here myself, just in case of a spot of bother. Never used the thing yet, in anger. Don't suppose I could hit the east end of a cow going west with it, even if I had to. But it's good for morale, you know. If we get out anywhere I'll just bring it along in case. What kind of guns do these birds have, any idea?"

Quarshie shook his head.

"Well, never mind. Have an idea we'll find out soon enough if we get within range."

Quarshie pointed ahead to what, if it had been in silhouette, might have been an iceberg in a wide expanse of ocean.

"That looks like our destination. What are we, twenty miles off?"

"More like forty, I'd say, old man." The pilot paused and then added after a moment's reflection, "Softly softly catchee monkee, eh?" Even to Quarshie's ear the man's idioms were curiously out of date, more as if they came from books than from conversation. "Don't want to sail in there and fly right down the barrel of a gun, do we? I suggest we close in to about a mile and then do a gentle circuit. Sound all right to you?"

Quarshie held his thumb up.

They had been airborne for almost an hour. He looked over his shoulder at his two assistants and hoped, from what he saw, that he was not going to have to call on either of them for any immediate action.

Twenty minutes later they started to fly around the great splintered pile of rocks.

On their second circuit the pilot pointed ahead and downwards. "Wheel tracks going north," he said. "We'll go in and take a closer look. But not too close, get nasty downdraughts between those chimneys in the rocks, there."

Mamadou was taking an interest again in his surroundings, and as they turned the eastern bastion of the rocks he tapped Quarshie's shoulder from behind and pointed downwards.

Almost out of sight in a cleft in the rocks there were some gasoline drums.

The pilot shook his head and spoke into his intercom: "I think the birds have flown. We should have seen some sign of life if there had been anyone around here. We flew over a lot of trodden sand on each side of a set of tyre marks back there. If we took off in the direction they were pointing, I think they would link up with those I saw going north a few minutes ago. Shall we put down and have a closer look or chase off and see if we can catch up with them?"

"Put down," Quarshie told him, partly because he thought Michel needed a little respite, but also because he wanted to see if they could find definite evidence that the place had been visited during the last twenty-four hours.

Quarshie felt that he had never known what peace, quiet and stillness were until after the pilot had landed and had switched off his engine. The wind which licked at them as they got out of the machine was like a tongue of fire.

Michel fell straight onto his knees as his feet touched the ground. He got up but staggered like a drunken man when he tried to walk, and Quarshie helped him to a place in the shade of the rocks where he could sit for a while and recover.

"This was obviously where they hung out, eh?" Sogo called out to Quarshie. "All very neat and tidy, though, like a dormitory in a barrack block. The brass must have run this outfit like a military camp."

Quarshie said, "You were right about their loading stuff here. The truck must have been fitted with lifting gear, see? They had the drums on their sides, rolled them to the tailgate, dug a hole in the sand to get a chain or rope around them, and then, maybe, hoisted them up."

Mamadou, who had been scouting out further from the rocks than the others, came back with a solemn expression on his long, narrow face, which was still an unnatural colour.

"Human bones out there," he told Quarshie. "They are laid out on a rock, three complete skeletons. This is a bad place, sir."

Michel heard Mamadou from where he was sitting and said in a weak voice, "The feel is of much evil." He had his eyes closed, his head back against the rock and his chin up in the air. "It is like a room in which a man is dying or dead. The true spirit has left the place and the *loups-garous* have moved in."

He stopped speaking. Quarshie gave him a few moments' silence and then asked, "Do you get anything else from the place?"

Michel took a very long time before he answered and they all waited, Sogo with his eyes very wide open and an expression on his face which suggested that he was not certain whether to believe what he heard or not. Looking at Michel, he experienced the feeling that he had withdrawn from them and perhaps even from his own body, which was left propped up against the rock like a discarded rag doll.

Michel's face ran with sweat, which curved along the line of his jaw and dripped off his chin.

His lips moved three or four times before any words came out. All three men drew closer to him.

"It is the same picture," he said. "Dust and fear and noise. And there are dead, too. I can't, not more. I can't." He opened his eyes and there was a puzzled expression in them. "But we must go on," he said, "we must go on. Because we are there. It will happen."

Sogo gestured to Quarshie to come away. Out of earshot of Michel, he asked anxiously, "What is he? Some sort of human radar?"

"Yes, some sort of radar . . . and very human because, unlike radar, he can feel what he sees—fear, pain, sorrow. It's a terrible gift."

"And what is he talking about?"

"I wish I knew . . . exactly. It means that we have to be doubly on the lookout because there is trouble ahead. But knowing that and being on the lookout for it, surely we should be able to avoid it."

"So we go on?"

"It's hard to turn back," Quarshie replied slowly, "on the evidence of a man who has second sight. Our ancestors would have turned back, of course, but . . . but we came here in a helicopter. We can talk to base on the R.T. I am a doctor of medicine, you are a pilot . . ." Quarshie kicked the sand with his toe and was about to continue when Mamadou joined them.

He said, "I have information, sir."

"Yes, Mamadou?"

"There is a dungheap just around the corner, sir. It has been used recently, and whoever was there left some sheets of newspaper that they had not used. It is the one my uncle publishes, and it has yesterday's date on it."

Quarshie smiled. "You are a much better detective than I am, my friend. Then they can only just have left. If we can pick up the trail we might catch them out in the open somewhere. We'll go after them. When we are airborne," he told Sogo, "you can call base and tell them to get that column which they have standing by, on the move out this way. Tell them it is top priority, that we are going to need them very soon, and since we have no arms . . . no . . . we will get airborne and then you will get me right through to the General. We cannot take any chances of things getting delayed. It's a pity there is not another helicopter or some other type of military aircraft we could call on."

As they got back into the machine Michel asked, "You don't believe what I told you, sir?"

"Indeed I do. It's because I do that we are going on. What you told me is what would have happened if you had not given me that warning. We are prepared now for whatever we may find, and can be doubly on guard against anything going wrong."

"You believe that you can alter whatever it is that fate has in store for you?"

Overhearing this question, Mamadou answered, "Nothing can befall us but what God has destined for us. Our liege Lord is He . . . and in God let the faithful trust."

Quarshie sighed quietly, so that it went unnoticed by the others, and thought the process of decision making became more complex when one was confronted by a man whose views, based on his religion, were that it was impossible to escape a preordained fate, and by another man who seemed to have the power to foretell what that fate was going to be.

THIRTEEN

We shall succeed.

No one had told Quarshie before he left Fort Etienne that Mrs. Quarshie was on her way to join him.

Nor did anyone, when she arrived, tell her that Quarshie was off hunting the leaders of the assassins in a helicopter.

With the French Ambassador from Akhana she had gone first to the local French Embassy, where they had pressed her to stay. She refused their offers of hospitality politely and very firmly. She wanted to be with her husband, she told them, and asked where he was staying.

When she heard that he was at the Hotel Buffet de la Gare, she asked the Ambassador to telephone the hotel and tell them to move another bed into his room. After he had made the call, the Ambassador came back and told her that Quarshie had gone out but that they would make the arrangements she had asked for.

With a look at the Ambassador, which he found quite easy to interpret, she said, "I will wait for him there. He will be surprised to see me. I expect he has missed me."

"As you, no doubt, have missed him, *chère Prudence*." They had travelled a long way together in an Embassy limousine, and for the first time in their association he had stopped calling her "*chère madame*" and had started calling her by her first name. "But why," he asked her, "an extra bed, why not just one big one? As a friend of the family I take the liberty to make such a suggestion, thinking, of course, only of the happiness of my dear Quarshie and his so beautiful wife."

"I do not consider it a liberty, sir, only your guilty conscience at work to put right the damage you have done in being the cause of our separation for such a long time."

"That you have missed him so much, Prudence, does you very

much credit." The old man bowed with mock gallantry. "I would, of course, have made the suggestion that I should have been allowed to take away the pain of loneliness by taking the good Doctor's place in your arms, had I not known that you would refuse me, *à l'instant.*"

"And, of course, your judgement was exactly right, sir."

It was a game. The Ambassador had made his play by his mock gallantry, and Mrs. Quarshie had countered his move by sounding prim.

Now, as it came to his move again, the Ambassador made a gesture of resignation and sighed, "The price one pays for being right is often too much, much too much. If I were a young man again I would make it more difficult for you to dismiss my *cour*—how you say it? my *proposition*—so easily. Now, however, there is nothing for me to do but to drive you to your hotel"—he paused dramatically—"and to leave you all alone at the door."

Quarshie's room, to which the second bed had not yet been delivered, possessed a number of items which spoke at once to Mrs. Quarshie of her husband.

There was a gaily coloured tie-dyed shirt, which she had bought for him, hanging over the back of a chair. On the table beside the bed there was a photograph of her with their adopted son Arimi. There was a red silk dressing gown with the name of a French fashion designer in the collar band. She had found it by chance in a Kingsway store when she had been looking for some socks for Arimi. And on the dressing table there was the leather briefcase she had chosen for him from a catalogue she had sent for from an expensive English store.

She opened the briefcase and found a thick exercise book bearing the title *Diary of the Fort Etienne Assassinations . . . for Prudence.* At once she sat down to read it.

The sheet of paper with the note on it that Quarshie had written for her before he left, was folded in half and inserted loose at the back of the book, and she only found it after she had read the rest of the diary.

For a moment she sat stunned and motionless. Then she started to move and did not stop, though several people tried to detain her, until she was sitting in a chair facing the General's Chef de Cabinet. Being a percipient man, he too surrendered to her insistence that she see the General, knowing that he, and only he, would have the calm authority to reduce Mrs. Quarshie's disquiet and satisfy her need for reassurance.

It was fortunate too that, only minutes after she had entered the General's office, Quarshie's voice had come in on the loudspeaker installed in there, reporting to the General on the details of their search of Alamut and his plans to follow the wheel tracks in the desert away towards the north. It had all sounded very routine and as if Quarshie was taking every possible precaution, and Mrs. Quarshie had returned to a state of mind that was almost normal.

Soon after the helicopter took off from the assassins' first camp, Quarshie spoke carefully over the intercom to the military base in Fort Etienne and to the General.

"The leaders of the operation against the Fort Etienne whites," he said, "have abandoned their base and are headed deeper into the desert. Here, there is considerably more sand, and although they appear to be trailing some device designed to obliterate their wheel tracks, the ruts left by the truck are often quite clear and we are having very little difficulty in following them. Captain Sogo tells me we are steering a course that varies between zero nine degrees and fourteen degrees. Our departure point was a jebel called Ba Allish and we are flying approximately parallel to Wadi Azoun, which is a couple of miles to the west. Our heading should bring us to other jebels along the southern fringe of the Ulad é Kaje escarpment. Since we are virtually unarmed and those we are pursuing, according to the girls we have captured, have several guns, when we do overtake them we shall stay out of range and wait for the support you are sending, so please despatch them as soon as possible. We know that one of the trio is a veteran of the war in Vietnam, so we can expect that he will be able to set up some kind of militarily effective defensive position. In terrain which offers as little cover as this, any attacking force will be badly exposed to small-arms fire. We will inform you as soon as we make contact with these people."

With the heat abating, the helicopter was less affected by the thermals which rose like geysers from every large rock that was not covered by sand. For this reason the motion of the machine was slightly less uncomfortable, and Michel and Mamadou were not quite so distressed by it.

A new sound in the machine disturbed Quarshie and he looked around and found that it came from Sogo, who was singing.

Presently the pilot stopped and told Quarshie, "If we have to go very much further we shall not be able to stay around wherever they happen to be for very long. That is, unless we come down and wait for base to send us more fuel. In any case, it would probably be more effective to fly back, fill the tanks, lift some more fuel with us and come back here again. Look"—he pointed ahead—"the first of the jebels, and you can see the é Kaje scarp behind them."

The Big M came out of his sleep very quickly with the sound of the chopper in his ears. It was instinct more than reason which told him what the noise indicated, and it was instinct again which made him reach for the MAT49 and slip a magazine into place. However, by the time he came out of the cave and into the cleft in the rock which led up to it, he saw the helicopter flying away and then saw it turn to the left and disappear behind a shoulder of rock. It must have been some distance off, he concluded, as it had come abreast of their hiding place. Too far to be within effective range of the sub-machine gun. A rookie might open fire at that distance, but not a man who had seen as much blood spilt as he had.

In the helicopter they had seen the tracks of the truck leading up towards the jebel, and had followed them until they had disappeared amongst the shale which was scattered around the base of the cliffs. They had not seen the drift of sand that led into the wedge-shaped opening in the rock where Arrani had parked the truck.

On their first wide sweep around the outcrop they had been looking for wheel tracks leading away from it and had not seen any.

"I'm going in a bit closer," Sogo told Quarshie.

The Big M kept his head down until he heard the chopper quite close, then he took a quick look and ducked again. Still too far out. Better to take a chance and let them land somewhere, if that was what they planned to do, than to give away his position. So he held his fire.

Mamadou, who was sitting behind the pilot, said, "There was a split in the rock in that place we just passed. I think I saw the lorry in there."

"Right. We'll do one more circuit, then land around the back and do a search on foot. O.K., Doc?"

Quarshie nodded.

From the way the sound reverberated as it reached him the third time, the Big M knew that his target would be closer to the rock on this approach than it had been before.

When he came out from behind the cover of the rocks it was a "right on" shot and he did what only a man of his immense strength could have done: he put the gun to his shoulder and sighted it steadily, standing with his legs wide apart. His target was the pilot, but he allowed a little deflection to compensate for the helicopter's speed.

As he fired, some pieces flew off the engine cowling behind the cabin, and at the end of the burst he thought he saw some fragments of metal falling away from a point near the tail rotor.

Sogo's reaction to the sound of bullets striking his machine was very swift. "Mayday. Mayday." He had his radio over onto transmit and was calling into his microphone: "We are under fire and have been hit repeatedly. Mayday. I am having trouble maintaining direction and stability. Will have to make a forced landing. Location first jebel on course from Ba Allish. Mayday."

He somehow got the helicopter around to the other side of the rock pile before the fuselage started to swing sickeningly and giddily in a circle beneath the main rotor. On the third gyration he put the machine down in a soft patch of sand a mile out from the west side of the jebel, cutting his engine at the same moment. The helicopter dropped, spinning like a car in a violent skid, and came to rest with a shriek of tearing metal and in a smothering fog of sand.

Then for a moment there was silence.

It was broken by Michel's choking voice as he cried, "I'm covered in blood. But I'm not bleeding. It's Mamadou. It's Mamadou." His voice went up in pitch. "He has fallen across my knees and he is bleeding all over me."

Mamadou was dead.

And the helicopter had started to burn a few minutes after it had crashed.

Quarshie had lifted his young assistant out of the seat and had carried him in his arms to the cover of a reef of rocks nearby, but since they had had to put the reef between them and a possible attack from the jebel, he had had to lay him on the sunny side of the rocks. Though this fact was of no consequence, because it was a lifeless body that Quarshie had laid gently down in the sand.

Michel and Sogo had had time to remove a jerrycan full of water, some emergency desert rations, the Captain's revolver, and a small box of ammunition before the flames drove them to follow Quarshie into cover.

For a while the three survivors were silent as they lay on the sandy-floored bay amongst the rocks which Quarshie had chosen for their retreat. The surprise of the gunfire and the events which had followed it had struck so suddenly that their actions thereafter had had the unreality of movements made by men unexpectedly caught in a condition of weightlessness. And their return to reality came slowly through the kind of haze which drifts through a man's mind as he regains consciousness after having been deeply anaesthetised.

Mamadou had been hit by two bullets. One of them, jagged and tumbling after having passed through the metal fuselage, had struck him in the windpipe and had continued on to rupture his jugular vein. A second had hit the hinge of his jaw, and Quarshie presumed that it had lodged somewhere in the lower lobes of his brain.

Both he and Michel were coated with the dead man's blood.

Sogo was the first to speak.

He said, "We are lucky that there are three out of the four of us alive and unhurt." Then, seeing misery on Quarshie's face, he said, so that it sounded almost like an apology, "I'll get into cover over there"—he pointed to the side of the reef nearest to the jebel—"and keep an eye open for anyone coming this way." He broke his revolver and spun the chambers with his thumb to check that they were loaded, and crouching to remain under cover, he moved away.

Quarshie made an enormous effort and dragged himself back from a state of mental limbo in which there was only pain. It was a state in which he could think only of the fact that he had been the cause of Mamadou's death.

Now his mind shifted to a different level of awareness.

The man who had killed Mamadou must have already been party to the deaths of all those who had been murdered with the garrotte—the child, the old missionary, the young welder, all of them. He had had no personal contact, this killer, with any of those who had been killed because, in his megalomaniacal mind, he had taken to himself the right to remove life at any time from anyone, satisfying some belief that he had the right to commit murder in the name of . . . what? And did a man who manifestly denied the right to live to those whom he chose to kill arbitrarily, without trial, argument, or established reason, have any right to be left with his own life?

Quarshie felt a power growing in him that was as exceptional as the wickedness of the man he would now confront . . . and kill. He was not concerned, any more with any sort of ideology but with the eradication of a malignant disease which called itself "terrorism" and against which there was no antidote except, as in the case of gangrene, amputation. That was it. The three must be removed before their infection spread any further.

Quarshie looked at Michel, who was not quite sure how to read the look except that he knew that the power and purpose that the Big M had had before had been raised to a very great heat and that he had made an irrevocable decision.

Very quietly Quarshie said, "We must leave Mamadou here and cover him with rocks so that the vultures will not get to him. Then we must go and find the man who killed him. We will go soon after sunset. You see better than other men in the dark. You will lead the way. We will find this murderer and his friends and kill them if they do not surrender."

The Big M had seen the smoke from the burning helicopter when he had climbed the ridge behind his hideout to look over the hill. There was no sign of life around the machine or between it and the jebel. If there were any survivors and they made the unlikely choice of delivering an immediate counterattack, they would have to cover better than two and a half miles to reach the cave.

The smoke made by the burning fuel in the helicopter hid the tracks in the sand, which led from the wreck to the rocks, from his view.

He was not prepared to assume for certain that everyone had perished, but he felt that there was a good chance that they were either dead or too seriously injured to be in any way active.

Calculating his next move, he reckoned that the men in the helicopter could well have given the position of his new camp to their base. He knew that, even if the authorities in Fort Etienne had an emergency force ready to take off in hot pursuit, he had much better than twenty-four hours' lead. Darkness would be falling very soon. The desert ahead of them was unreconnoitred. There were crevasses in the rocks which would not show up in the truck's headlights, so they had to travel by day. They needed more rest and food.

He could not overlook the possibility, however, that if any of those aboard the helicopter had survived they might move in . . . but surely not before daylight, since they were strangers to the terrain. It could not be more than one chance in a hundred that they would make a night attack, yet he must guard against that one chance.

The others were waiting for him below, having been wakened by the gunfire. He decided that they would eat again now, and then, while he and Arrani got more sleep, Kali could stand guard, since she could not drive the truck. Then, at first light, they would set out on a long drive. They were self-contained. They had food, fuel and water. To the east, according to the map, there were wide areas of desert, made up mostly of rock and shale, where the truck would leave no trail.

It was a pity that they would have to move again so quickly, but that was the price which had to be paid in a guerilla war.

As the three men moved quietly around the base of the jebel, Quarshie was still feeling outside the range of normal human potential. It was as if he had taken a drug that had not only increased the flow of adrenalin but had also increased the sensitivity and power of his mind.

He knew that they were fortunate that the moon would rise late.

He knew that their first objective must be the truck. It must be put out of action so that the man he had to kill would not escape him.

He knew, above all else, that he would be successful and that Michel's vision of the death of a big man did not apply to him but to one of those who opposed him.

The three men were walking in single file, with Michel leading. The latter kept to the sand, skirting rocks and boulders, and all three men were barefooted to make certain that they did not lose the vital feel of the ground.

Michel moved carefully but with confidence. He, too, now shared Quarshie's view of what lay ahead, as if his mind had become an extension of the Doctor's.

Presently Sogo, who was following closely on Michel's heels, touched him on the shoulder. The pilot and Mamadou had been sitting on the inside of the turn as they had flown around the jebel, so they were the ones who had seen the rock formation most clearly.

Sogo pointed ahead and said, "The place the gunfire came from is just around the corner." And he wondered if the error of judgement which had brought them so close to the enemy would be thought of as his fault or Quarshie's. At once he shrugged the thought aside, not being given to worrying over his own or other people's mistakes.

Quarshie and Sogo stopped in the deep darkness of an overhanging bluff and Michel went on by himself, with the same sinuous grace with which he moved his slender body as he sang.

The two men he left behind strained their eyes to watch him as he slipped in and out of the blackest shadows and then dropped to his knees as he reached the spit of rocks which shelved down into the sand.

After that, they did not see him for twenty minutes, and he surprised them, when he did reappear, by slipping out of the darkness under another bluff that was quite close to them.

He beckoned to them to sit down and in the clear, pale light of the stars he drew a rough plan in the sand of the V-shaped entrance to the cleft in the cliff in which the truck was parked.

"The woman is on guard and she has a gun. I was able to get quite close to her. The truck will be visible from almost any place in the V. I suggest, sir, that you follow the trail I left in the sand. It will take you behind several rocks and you will come to a stop almost immediately behind the woman. Then Captain Sogo and I will make a little noise out at the point of the rocks there. She will come to investigate—she only has to move a very little way—and you can take her from behind. At that moment the Captain and I will move to some big rocks which are out in the middle of the entrance here." He drew the rocks on his plan. "From there we shall be facing the truck and the only way the men can come out from behind it. Then the Captain will be able to shoot at them. If the woman does not move to see what caused the noise we shall make, perhaps you will be able to attack her anyway. She will be quite close and is fat and will move slowly.

"Also, you told me before I left that it is necessary to make sure that the truck cannot be moved. It is backed into the narrow opening of the cave, perhaps to make it easy to unload it. From this place behind the rocks where we shall be, it will have to come directly towards us before it turns to go past us, and the Captain will be able to shoot straight at the driver. Is it a good plan, sir?"

Quarshie and Sogo considered the idea carefully for a few moments, Quarshie visualising every movement that Michel had suggested, as if he were looking at it on a film screen.

Sogo spoke first. He said, "If I see the situation correctly from here"—he pointed at the rocks to which he and Michel were to move—"all I have to do is fire some bullets into the thing's radiator.

And they would never get any distance with it in this heat before the engine seized up."

They both waited for Quarshie to comment. He had his eyes shut, and the power of his concentration was almost tangible.

Finally he said, "It is a good plan. It will work. Only if I get the woman before she makes any noise will you fire at the radiator, Sogo. We shall not be able to enter the cave in the dark and take the men. They will have to come out in the open. Your shooting will bring them out. I will leave the woman where she falls, after I have tied her up. I shall have her gun and I will get back into hiding here." He pointed to their map in the sand. "They may think she has been killed. They will not know where we are in hiding, how many of us there are, or how well we are armed. But we shall be where we can attack from the front, or the side. One point we shall all have to understand. We shall be lucky if the plan works the way we hope it will. We may have to make sudden changes. Sogo, you have the gun. Michel, you have the eyes. Later, but much later, we shall have the moon. It will light your rocks before it lights the face of this cliff where they are hiding. It is even possible that they have another man above us now on the cliffs, so be sure that your rocks give you cover from someone above you. Here"—he indicated the end of the spit of rocks—"we shall separate and may not make contact again until it is all over. Stay under cover, but call to me, Michel, if you see anything you think I should know. In a few hours we shall have finished the work we have to do. At the moment I think they have—what do they call it?—the firepower. We have the initiative, and we are not fighting to save our lives but to take theirs. We shall succeed."

As it happened, Michel and Sogo did not have to make any noise to attract Kali away from the front of the cave and further out into the desert. She walked forward a few steps of her own accord, so that Quarshie could take her from behind, his bare feet in the soft sand making his approach quite soundless. He made a sort of diving tackle, grasping her ankles with his hands at the same moment that his shoulder caught her just above the knees.

She had no way to fall but forwards and came down holding the Russian rifle across her midriff so that it knocked the wind out of her. At once Quarshie got on top of her with his knees on her shoulder blades. She had opened her mouth to cry out, but before she could make any sound Quarshie forced her face into the sand so that her open mouth was immediately filled with it.

So the whole event had taken place without a sound except her sudden intake of breath when he first struck her. Even the AK47 fell noiselessly into the sand.

He continued to press her face down with all his strength until her body stopped heaving beneath his knees. Then he took her headtie and used it to fasten her hands behind her back. The long cotton pants she was wearing had no belt but were held up with elastic. He removed them and tied the trouser legs around her shins and ankles. Though she had given up her struggles she was still breathing, so he turned her on her back and left her to fight to clear her nose and mouth of sand. As he picked up the gun he told her softly, "I shall only be a few yards away; if you make the least sound I will fire this thing at you, and I think you can be fairly sure that you will die." The confidence he felt did not, he realised, extend to firearms.

A few moments later, when Quarshie had disappeared back into the shadows, Sogo began to shoot at the truck's radiator. He fired five times, and three times Quarshie heard the zipping whine of bullets as they ricocheted off steel.

After that, there was no sound for a long time.

The sound of the first shot aroused the Big M, but he did not want to believe the evidence of his ears. His instinct told him that there should not be any sound of gunfire, and he accepted its suggestion for two or three seconds. Then Sogo fired again, and at once the Big M came fully alert. He shook Arrani awake and they listened in silence to the three shots which followed, hearing, as Quarshie had, the sound of the ricochets.

Thoughtfully the Big M said, "That's not the AK47. That's a handgun. Maybe they've got Kali. Maybe she couldn't stay awake and they jumped her." And as Arrani got hurriedly to his feet he cautioned him, "Take it easy, brother, don't stick your neck out. We've got to look around carefully. It could be that they figured on your doing just what you were going to do now—rush out there and right into an ambush. If they have any sense, and we've got to reckon that they have, they won't come in here after us. They think they've got us. And maybe they have. We look like we're trapped. That's how they've got it figured. And maybe we are, and maybe we ain't. Let's go see what gives, but carefully, brother, carefully. I'll get up in the truck and slit the canvas back of the cab. You crawl underneath it. That way nobody see us."

Arrani's mouth was dry and, for the first time since he had joined forces with Kali and the Big M, he was frightened.

"What can have happened to Kali?" he asked.

"Only one thing, I guess. She got hit. But they're not going to get us. Not as easily as they got her." The Big M moved towards the tail-board of the truck, which was already down. "Put the MAT49 up here with the M16," he added. "We won't need them yet. Yeah, like that. Good. Now, get down on the sand there and make like you're a snake and crawl through under the truck. Don't go no further forward than you need to, to be able to see, right?" And he climbed carefully and silently up onto the truck.

Equally carefully, he then worked the sharp point of his knife into the canvas curtain which hung from the truck's almost flat roof on all four sides. The place where he chose to make the slit was over the righthand side of the cab near the upright. When it was several inches long he opened it with his fingers and peered through it.

Unlike Arrani, he was not at all frightened. Death was not one of his enemies. He had taken its measure, knowing that he could often outwit it but that there would come a day when it would win. Every movement he made was deliberate and unflustered; every faculty he could muster was alert and tuned to as high a pitch of concentration as he could achieve.

In the starlight outside, everything was still, too still. The immobile lump in the centre of the estuary of sand had to be Kali, and he assumed she was dead.

He felt sorry for her, remembering the softness of her skin, her obedience and her loyalty to him.

"I'll settle a score or two for you, baby," he told her, moving his lips soundlessly to form the words, "before they get me . . . *if* they get me." Though it looked very much as if he were trapped, and he admitted it to himself, he did not admit that he was beaten.

Except for the sand and the rocks there was nothing else to be seen, but there had to be other things out there, he told himself, like men with guns.

Stalemate, he thought; you won't come in, and I won't come out. Anyway, who the hell are you? Maybe there had been a flying column following right up behind the chopper. Or maybe he had not hit the chopper as hard as he thought he had. Just hard enough to make them put it down, and then they had set it on fire to fool him. No, that could not be right. Nobody would set fire to an expensive piece of equipment just to use it as a decoy.

"Then, what goes on out there?" He whispered the words to himself. "I don't get it. Somebody is playing games. They kill Kali and leave her where we can see her. Why? Psychological warfare. That's not Transnigerian soldier stuff. But it could be doctor stuff. Quarshie. Yeah, but where did he come from? Did another chopper come in during the night? Arrani had said they only had one chopper in the whole country. It was a four-seater. I must have gotten at least one of them, or maybe two. That would make two against two. If there are only two, maybe the best thing to do would be to make a break for it."

Arrani touched him on the shoulder and he jumped, which angered him because it was not fear which caused him to react that way, only the intensity of his concentration, yet it might look as if . . .

"Well?" he asked shortly.

"They got Kali."

"Yeah, I can see that from here."

"They were shooting at the radiator. It's still dripping, and there is a patch of wet sand underneath it."

" 'They'? How do you know it's 'they'?"

"I don't. I just assumed that there is more than one of them."

"You saw nothing else?"

"Nothing."

"O.K. Let's do a little figuring." The Big M sat on the sack of money and patted it with his hand. "Maybe we could buy them off with some of this," he hazarded. "No. I think it's Quarshie out there. He's not for sale. Least, that's what they say. Besides, what's to stop him taking the money and then taking us in, anyway?"

Arrani had no ideas to offer.

Eventually the Big M said, "What's your attitude? You want to fight, or you want to quit?"

Arrani shrugged. "It will be the same both ways, won't it?" He had got back his composure and his faith in the Koran and predestination.

"Yeah. I guessed that might be how you would see it. Well, it sure as hell ain't the way *I* see it. No old soldier is going to die in front of a firing squad, or with a rope around his neck. But if it is really all the same to you, then maybe there is a way we can both get out."

"How's that?"

"You know how Che Guevara, or Mao—if it wasn't some other dude—saw it? He said, 'When you can take some action or mount some kind of offensive, it's smart to get the enemy to think you can't do a thing.' O.K.? So here's the trick: you go out and surrender, give yourself up. It has to be you, because I can handle guns better than you can. Then, while they have all their attention on you, I'll be able to get up on the roof of the truck, climb up from there onto that little bit of cliff above it, and keep right on going until I am way above them. My guess is that there is two, or at the most, three of them. We'll wait until the moon comes up. Then the rock face on this side will be black against it—black, like me. Then, if you can get them out in the moonlight a little ways, I will be able to pick them off with my old friend here." He tapped the butt of the M16. "As soon as you hear the first shot you dive for cover. Get out of my way and theirs, too. You've seen how I can shoot. Well?"

"And if they shoot *me* when you open up on them?"

"You said it yourself, brother. If we don't get away, we're dead, and we sure as hell won't get away unless we take some chances."

"And the radiator?"

"We'll find a way to fix that, and fast too, once we've got rid of them."

Arrani walked to the back of the truck and came back. He shrugged. "Why not?" he said. "I don't have any other ideas. Like you said, if there are only three of them out there, it could work. Yeah, I really suppose it could. How long do you think we shall have to wait for the moon to be right?"

"Could be an hour, maybe a little more. When it gets onto those rocks out there, across the end of the entrance . . . that'll be the time to make a move."

The three men waiting outside the cave found the inaction and having to be on the alert all the time a great strain, and Sogo actually slept briefly a couple of times. He was overweight and had had to exert an unusual amount of nervous and physical energy during the past few hours.

Quarshie wondered how, if he had to use it, he would fire the gun. He knew nothing about firearms and disliked them. The others would not know that, of course, so if they saw him carrying it they might be intimidated. Amongst Africans a gun was not a traditional weapon for killing. It made indiscriminate murder too simple, although the black man was learning fast the techniques of random killing that were made possible by Russian and American supplies of arms.

However, during most of the time he waited, he fought to maintain his resolve to kill the man who had shot Mamadou. That character certainly knew how to use a gun, Quarshie thought, so he must be the man who, according to the reports Mamadou had found in the newspaper morgue, had been in Vietnam.

He was troubled, going over the whole thing again in his mind, like a sleepless man nagged by some critical anxiety in the middle of the night, when he heard a voice shouting, "I am coming out to surrender. I have no gun or any other weapon, and I am coming out to surrender."

Quarshie bit his tongue to cut back an instinctive response. He must remain concealed until he understood what was behind this new move.

Arrani walked very slowly out of the cave with his hands up and waving a piece of white cloth.

Quarshie made a great effort to project the warning he wanted to give to the others without shouting it.

It could be a ruse, because both men had not come out together.

Sogo started to stand up holding his gun on Arrani, but, as if he had read Quarshie's mind, Michel pulled the Captain down into the cover of the rocks again.

"Tell him to walk towards us here and to keep his hands up," Michel told his companion, "and watch him, because I have to watch . . ." And at that moment he saw the vague shape of a man on the roof of the truck. For a moment Michel hesitated; then, when he saw the man starting to climb the cliff with his back towards Michel's position, he ran, doubled up, across the sand to Quarshie.

"There is a man going up the rocks at the back there. I can't see him very well but he seems to be a very big man," he told the Doctor.

Quarshie studied Michel's face without knowing that he was doing it, trying to read something, trying to see ahead.

"Yes. Yes, I think it is the man . . . I feel it is the man. It's like a faint sound, or a faint smell, but it is inside my head. I am sure . . . really . . . now . . . I'm sure."

Quarshie gave him the gun, saying, "I don't need this." And he moved back along the spit of rocks, out of sight of the cave mouth, and started to climb the rocks on a line that would take him parallel to a direct ascent from the mouth of the cave.

Michel ran back across the sand to the cover of the rocks where

Sogo was holding Arrani at gunpoint. He wanted to be able to watch the progress of the man on the face of the cliff.

Looking back over his shoulder for a moment, the Big M saw Michel dart across the sand and disappear behind the rock he and Sogo were using for cover. "So that's where you are," he said softly. "Well, I'm not ready yet, but I'll get you when I am. The boot is going to be on the other foot now. I'm going to pin you down like you thought you had me pinned down."

He was, of course, unaware of Quarshie, barely a hundred yards away, climbing with him.

Quarshie's intention, as he clambered higher, was a typically military one, though he did not think of it that way. It was to get the advantage of ground over his enemy, to be above him.

Unlike Quarshie, the American was climbing carelessly, occasionally setting a few stones loose to rattle down the slope.

In fact, the Big M, overconfident, now that he believed that he had the measure of his attackers, was scrambling both higher and sideways towards the south. He was moving as fast as he could, excited by the feeling that he was once again in a commanding position, oblivious to the noise he was making. It was this carelessness which gave Quarshie, climbing soundlessly, the ability to gauge his position in relation to that of his quarry.

When he paused to rest for a moment, he thought of Mrs. Quarshie. He would, he hoped, be seeing her quite soon, and he was more afraid of that encounter than he was of the one which lay immediately ahead of him. In his next meeting with her he was going to have to justify to her, and thus to himself, the fact that he had deliberately killed another human being . . . because he knew without any doubt that that was what he was going to do.

With an effort he pushed his picture of her out of his mind, afraid it might weaken his resolve. His decision had not been made in a moment of weakness, but out of the strength he had felt, born of his love and respect for Mamadou.

Suddenly it occurred to Quarshie that his quarry might add Michel to his list of victims, and he knew that his love for the albino was just as great.

And again he felt the surge of power that had gripped him when Mamadou had been killed.

He was sweating and shaking from his unusual exertion. Then he stopped climbing and listened.

There was no sound now coming from the position on the left where he had heard the clatter of the man's gun a few moments before.

With even greater caution he climbed another twenty or thirty feet and began to work towards the south. He was breathing heavily and having to be careful of the noise he made as he inhaled and exhaled.

Now, as he moved sideways across the shoulder of the ridge, checking each handhold and foothold before he put his weight on it, he looked down below him. Though the desert and the rocks at the entrance of the cleft were in the moonlight, it seemed to him as if the downward sweep of the jebel was in greater darkness than it had been before and he could see nothing of the American, no matter how fiercely he strained his eyes to penetrate the darkness.

And then there came an anticlimax.

Almost immediately below him the killer came incautiously to his feet and stood upright, with the upper part of his body silhouetted against the moonlit stretches of the desert.

Quarshie froze, trying to flatten himself more closely into the side of the hill, in case the man turned round and looked in his direction.

The Big M turned, however, only to his right and left, seeking perhaps a better position, then he sank back out of sight.

Quarshie moved slowly forward, tensed all the time to leap at his enemy in case he turned and saw him behind him.

When he reached the brink of the small ledge which had cut the man's body in two when he had stood up, the Doctor found that he was right above the American, who was spread out on the ground on his belly with his legs wide apart and his gun cradled against his cheek. Looking in the direction in which the rifle was pointing, Quarshie saw that they had outflanked the protective cover which the rocks below had given to Michel, Sogo and Arrani, and all three were in clear view.

He also saw that he had to attack at once.

He estimated the distance and direction and, from a crouch, jumped, aiming to land with both his knees in the small of the man's back. At the same time he reached for the man's neck with both his hands.

Quarshie felt a terrible pain in one knee and a jarring shock in the other, and the gun pitched upwards and exploded.

FOURTEEN

. . . a new Quarshie legend . . .

"I landed from a height of about four feet with one knee in the lumbar region of his back. With the other knee I hit a rock against which he had pressed his body . . ." Quarshie tapped his leg, which was in plaster. "That is the reason for this. I cracked my patella. Later the pain was terrible, though I was hardly conscious of it at the time. The momentum of my jump carried me over his head towards the edge of the shelf on which he was lying.

"As I pitched forward I got my hands around his neck. With his head somewhere under my stomach . . . I took him with me. For a few moments, as I hung onto him, we slithered down a slope; he remained underneath me with his face ground into the rocky surface of the hillside by my weight. We had started a landslide of small rocks, some of which stayed under us, and they lubricated our descent of the steep scree which, I could see, ended in a cliff.

"Then I rolled off him and clawed myself around so that my head was towards the top of the slope. Frantically I clutched at handholds which, at first, reduced the speed of my descent and eventually arrested it. There was a small ledge to my right and, flat on my belly, I inched myself sideways towards it. When I reached it I looked back. He had disappeared.

"I assume the blow he got from my knee must have struck his spine and temporarily paralysed his legs. Also, the way my weight on the back of his head brutalised his face must have added enormously to the shock of my attack and, at least partially, deprived him of his wits. In that condition he must have arrived at the edge of the cliff and been unable to stop himself from plunging over it.

"From the ledge I was able to call down to Michel and Sogo. They at once tied their prisoners up, found a rope in the back of the truck and came to help me.

"Eventually we made a very slow descent because of my knee . . ." He looked at it, patted the plaster and shrugged, dismissing it. "The next morning," he continued, "I hobbled around the jebel and did a crude autopsy on the Big M, as his gang call him. He had dropped over the cliff and had fallen on his head, from a height of about a hundred feet, onto a wide rock which had an almost flat surface.

"Even the cheerful Sogo was silent when we first found the wretched man's remains. Evidence of the destructibility of the human skull was spread over a wide area. There was no way of telling whether he was already dead before he hit the rock. If he was not, there could be no doubt that death struck at the same instant that his head hit the rock."

Quarshie was sitting with his left leg stuck out in front of him and with a walking stick leaning against the arm of his chair.

At the moment he was the centre of attention and would have very much preferred not to be.

His real need was to be alone with Mrs. Quarshie.

Other wounds besides his cracked kneecap were raw and painful, and he needed her touch, her love, her common sense to heal them.

Nevertheless, he had been honour bound to fulfill the obligation of a visit to the General. With Quarshie and his host in the old man's office were Mrs. Quarshie and the Chef de Cabinet.

"About forty-eight hours later the army arrived and picked us up and brought us back here, where we handed over our prisoners to the police." And there had been the joy of finding Mrs. Quarshie waiting for me, he had wanted to add. Instead he concluded, "I don't think that there should be any lack of evidence against the Big M's two lieutenants. I have dictated everything I know about the case and handed over all the oddments of physical evidence that I have to the police, though I have kept a copy of Langston Hughes' poem—the one about 'Death is a drum . . . beating forever'—as a memento of the fact that we succeeded in stopping the beating of one drum."

It was the end of his story.

There followed a long silence.

Mrs. Quarshie and the Chef de Cabinet, following protocol, waited for the General to speak first.

Finally, the old man said rather ponderously: "The important conclusions we come to usually involve us in troublesome choices, and afterwards we keep asking ourselves, Did I do right or wrong?"

The Chef de Cabinet, who had been bitter about Mamadou's death, looked surprised. The words were not those he had expected to hear from the General. Both Quarshie and Mrs. Quarshie knew at once what had prompted the General's observation. "As head of state, self-questioning often involves me in passing judgements on my decisions, which could, if I let them, lean with unbearable weight on my soul. I know that you are troubled about Mamadou. Your concern about his death has been an undertone to everything you have told us. You are assuming that you were responsible for his death. You should remember, perhaps, that it was I who made him your assistant. I wanted you to have the best help we could give you. You said he had become a son to you. He was my son, too. I watched him grow up. I knew what the future could hold for him. Surely, too, you must realise that you are the only person anywhere in the world who will question whether what you did is right or wrong." And there was a glint of anger in the General's eye as he looked across at his Chef de Cabinet as if he were challenging him to deny that statement. "To most people it was clear that you were risking your own life, right beside Mamadou, to free our people from a vengeful gang who had been fighting an undeclared war on us. And you won. So you are a hero. Unhappily, however, where men turn to violence, death is always the only real victor."

The General's silvery head gleamed as he turned and looked directly at the Doctor. He patted Quarshie on the arm and said, "Words don't help much on these occasions, I know. For a man of conscience, good actions will never absolve him, in his own view, from those that he sees as bad ones." Then he frowned and continued: "As you spoke I thought that perhaps I also heard you saying that you felt that you were in the wrong to have brought about the death of the ruffian who led the gang. Let me tell you, my friend, when any man kills a terrorist his action will always be justified. Rather, people will sing your praises and a new Quarshie legend will be born. You questioned your own impulsiveness, and I tell you that it is irrelevant whether it was your heart or your mind which was in control of your actions when you attacked that man and killed him, whether you were avenging Mamadou or—your word, I think, was 'amputating' a terminally cancerous element of our society."

Quarshie looked unconvinced.

"He's obstinate, isn't he?" the General said to Mrs. Quarshie. Turning back to Quarshie he commanded, "Come with me to the window."

Quarshie struggled awkwardly to his feet and followed the General to one of the tall windows, which framed a sun-scorched view of parched land, craggy boulders, soilless hills, and the black scribble of the river.

A tiny puff of wind stirred the dry leaves of a "brown paper" tree just outside the window, and it rustled as if to explain the reason for its having been given its name.

"I am not extemporising for your benefit, my friend," the General told Quarshie. "I am taking you through a drill I go through myself every time I question one of my own decisions to the point where I find it hard to live with it myself. Those rocky hills out there, so a visiting geologist told me, are *three hundred million* years old. It is an important fact to remember and it helps me to remember my own insignificance—even though, with the help of others, I rule several million people. It helps me to turn an objective eye on my subjective concern as to whether I have made a good decision or a bad one. Doctor, we all spend too much of our lives struggling to find the right responses to transitory questions, because it satisfies our vanity to feel that we can find what, in the end, can only be equally transitory responses."

With a change of tone he said, "My Chef de Cabinet and I have been exercising our minds on another problem, a very difficult one. It is how we should reward a modest man such as you are. It is impossible to measure the work you have done for us and our people. You will, of course, accept some payment for your time and your expenses, but that is not what we have been talking about. We decided in the end to offer you something rather insignificant but something, we hope, you will find meaningful." The old man took a broad gold ring off one of his fingers. "This," he said, handing it to Quarshie, "is one of a number of relics of the past which go with the office of President. It is said to have been made during the Askia dynasty. I speak in the name of all Transnigerians when I say we want you to have it. Hoping that you would not refuse it, I have taken the liberty of having the year it is presumed to have been made and the present year inscribed inside it. It is, I believe, a little over four hundred years old. Besides reminding you of our gratitude, it will also, perhaps, help to keep Mamadou's memory alive for you, something I am sure he would wish."

Quarshie tried to reply but found that he was almost speechless. He could only look at the ring on his finger and mumble unintelligibly about being "honoured and grateful" while the General smiled, accepting his inarticulate sentences as a more serious acknowledgement of the gift and the feeling behind it than any well-expressed words could have conveyed.

Mrs. Quarshie said, "If you asked an independent and unbiased person, he would tell you that you are merciful to other people to a fault and merciless on yourself. I am not afraid of you, or for you, because I know that there is nothing in you that anyone needs to fear. You say that you lost control of yourself. So what were you doing in that 'moment of blindness'? You were saving the lives of Michel and Sogo. Do you really expect to be able to kill a man in cold blood with your bare hands, a man who had killed a valuable young friend and was about to kill another? And if you had found that you could have done it in cold blood, would that satisfy you?"

They were standing on the upstairs verandah outside their bedroom in a house which belonged to the Chef de Cabinet.

Mrs. Quarshie's gentle sympathy and concern for the man's sorrow over his nephew's death had turned a potential enemy into a remarkably considerate friend who had suggested that the Quarshies should have a holiday in a house he owned which had once belonged to the French Governor-General in the Transniger protectorate.

It had been a hot-weather residence and it looked out over the Niger a couple of hundred miles south of Fort Etienne.

The French Ambassador to Akhana had dropped them there, saying that he would come back to fetch them in a week. He had taken Michel to stay with him while arrangements were being made to send him abroad to study music. He would return with the Ambassador, when the Frenchman came to fetch them, then stay with the Quarshies until all the arrangements had been completed for him to go to Europe or America on a special scholarship grant.

Quarshie said, "In a curious way I seem to have made death my business, first as a doctor and now as . . ."

"A man who does everything he can to save people from death by violence," Mrs. Quarshie interposed quickly and firmly. In a softer voice she said, "Quarshie, if you weren't so big, or if I were bigger, I would shake you to get all this glooming and mooning out of you."

The house stood right on the bank of the river and they could hear the water, now very low, gurgling between some rocks on the riverbed.

In the darkness the lights from a window across on the other bank sent silvery snakes of fire darting across the shallows towards them.

"Of course you are right, Prudence." Quarshie put his arm around his wife's waist. "And of course there is another way by which you can always make me forget everything . . . except you. That is . . . if you don't think this plaster will get in the way."

With a snuffly giggle she asked, "Does what you are referring to have its roots in your mind, your heart, or, what do they call it, that thing, your manhood?"

"All of them," Quarshie replied. "Intellect, heart and manhood."

"Leaving nothing on those rocks out in the desert?"

As she asked the question, Mrs. Quarshie knew she was making a mistake.

Quarshie's hands were behind her back and he felt the broad band of gold around one finger with the thumb of the same hand.

"Nothing." It was a lie, but he wanted to please her.

She did not believe him though she accepted his response, telling herself, "There must be no ghosts, no ghosts. There must only be Quarshie and me."

And later she knew, when he was asleep beside her, that she had at least won a temporary victory, and was convinced that she would in the end go on and win any war, however protracted, because she would never share him with anyone, or with memories, or with any spirits of the dead.